First Wolf

Carole Anne Carr

Carole Anne Carr

16.02.09

For my husband with love

Cover design by James Brinkler

info@jamesbrinkler.co.uk

Published by Carole Anne Carr

thecakeandcustardbookshop.co.uk

Printed by MPG Biddles Ltd.

24 Rollesby Rd, King's Lynn, PE30 4LS

ISBN: 978-0-9559818-0-7

Contents

One – A Dangerous Hearth Lord

Two – Escape to the Forest

Three – Wolf Attack

Four – No One to Celebrate

Five – In the Rubbish Pit

Six – High Tide at the Crossing Place

Seven – The Hermit on Inner Farne

Eight – Kendra the Slave Girl

Nine – A Dragon on the Beach

Ten – A Promise Not Kept

Eleven – Widsith the Minstrel

Twelve – Trapped in the Dungeons

Thirteen - The Return of the King

Fourteen - At Dudda's Tavern

Fifteen - The White Church

ONE

A Dangerous Hearth Lord

It was my twelfth year of life when my father Godwin hurled the wolf's head at the mighty Eorl Uhtred, bringing my childhood to a violent end.

The cold woke me early on that terrible day. My three-year-old brother Rinan, curled up like a dormouse beside me, had taken most of the sheepskin covers, and I was angrily moving into my brother's warm patch when I heard the door latch click and father calling to someone as he hurried from the house.

These were dangerous times, and desperate to find out what was happening, I forgot grandmother asleep behind the woollen hangings, but hearing no angry grunt from her, and making as little noise as possible, I dragged on my trousers. Feeling about in the straw for my woollen tunic, I quickly pulled it over my linen one and fastened my belt. Then lifting my useless leg over the side of the low wooden bed, I tugged on my boots without bothering to undo the strings, and struggled awkwardly to my feet.

Only a few shafts of light came through the smoke hole in the thatched roof, and it was hard to find my way through the house. After the bitterly cold night, the oiled skins hung at the window places, and I shuffled across the floor, banged my legs on a stool, and gasped with

1

pain.

Terrified I'd disturbed grandmother I kept very still, hardly daring to breathe. Waking her without good reason would mean no hare coursing with Bodo, and days spent on the heath gathering herbs. Thankfully, the goat tethered in straw at the far end of the room did not start her shrill bleating, and the hens, roosting on beams above me, crooned softly and settled in their feathers.

My lurcher hound Bodo lifted his head, his eyes glittering in the light from the glowing embers in the sand box. I was worried he might bark, but he gave a long sigh, and deciding it was too soon to be up he returned to his watchful slumber, and I lifted the door latch and slipped quietly out of the house.

Limping between our neighbours' homes and workshops in the grey light of dawn, a sudden squealing made me jump, and at the end of the path, I saw the palisade doors wide open and our slaves driving animals in from the fields. Frightened pigs came squealing across the plank bridge into the yard, and a flock of sheep tore after them, their hooves pattering on the icy ground. Our shepherd cursed and roared for help as he chased the darting animals into the pens, and I shuffled away from the heavy oxen pounding fast towards me and felt their foggy breath warm and damp on my skin.

Our terrified beasts thumped against the high walls of our palisade, and my kinsmen shouted and struggled to trap them inside the hurdles. I was sure the hill tribes were on their way to slaughter us, and it seemed forever before my father Godwin ordered the gates closed and the wooden blocks lifted into the iron brackets.

With this done I felt safer, although I was still anxious to ask my father what was happening, and I waited impatiently while he gave many orders to the slaves, picked up a rotting wolf's head from the steaming midden, and came to greet me.

'Up so early, Toland?' my father said in his deep booming voice, his beard wagging, and his breath a thin cloud of white mist about his large head.

'Is it the hill tribes?' I asked nervously, looking up at him. I tried not to sound scared, but the words tumbled out and it was hard to keep fear from my voice. 'Are they going to attack?'

'Not the hill tribes this time. It's Uhtred, the king's nephew, with his household bodyguards. He thought to surprise us whilst we slept.' He gave a short laugh. 'I knew he would pay us a visit, now the king is gone from Bamburgh. See, I have a gift for the Eorl.'

He gave a wicked grin and dangled the wolf's head by its ear, close to my face. The stinking thing was almost as frightening in death as in life, but telling myself dead things couldn't hurt me, I looked into the empty eye sockets, at the blackened tongue lolling from its gaping jaws, and the deep split in the maggot-filled skull.

I didn't want father to see how I loathed the thing, and I pretended to laugh and patted it on the snout. This seemed to please him, for he gripped my shoulder with his fist in a kindly way. Then despite his giant size, he pounded up the nearest ladder and sprang lightly onto the raised walkway around the top of the palisade.

3

Filled with a fearful excitement, I was eager to watch Uhtred crossing the heath and to find out how many men rode with him. I'd seldom seen the Eorl, but I'd heard stories about this fearsome warrior. Hurrying to a ladder, I took most of my body weight with my arms that had grown strong because of my poor leg and climbed easily. Pulling myself onto the uneven planks of the walkway, I heard muttering and saw my brother Rinan talking excitedly to himself and climbing up towards me, his bare feet slipping dangerously on the rungs.

'Get down,' I scolded him. 'I'll tell father.'

Strong, and wilful for his years, Rinan took no notice. He reached the top of the ladder and made a grab for the walkway, but he wobbled dangerously, and I snatched at the back of his cloak and hauled him through the air. Then dumping him beside me, I heard father bellowing the call to arms.

Seizing Rinan's hand, I hurried him along the platform so fast his feet hardly touched the planks, and he wriggled and tried to kick me. It was then I saw my father fling the wolf's head high into the air and it landed with a soft thud on the far side of the newly dug earthworks, right in the path of Eorl Uhtred's horse.

The piebald side-stepped, rolling its liquid eyes in fear, and the Eorl cursed, savagely spinning the animal in a tight circle and bringing it to stand obedient and quivering before our gates. Moments later the Eorl's household bodyguards reigned in their lathered ponies beside him, their steaming mounts moving restlessly on the far side of the ditch.

They were near enough for me to see their scarlet armbands, worn over their leather tunics showing their rank, and their close fitting helmets. Each man carried a shield painted with a snarling bear, the Eorl's emblem, and held a light throwing spear. They were ready for battle, but they were small in number, and thinking we would easily defend our settlement against them, I heard shouting in the yard and saw my kinsfolk running to the gates.

Our archers were pushing and shoving to be first to climb the ladders. Leaping onto the walkway, they raced towards me, their feet thundering in the hollow space beneath the planks. Then jostling for position, they trained their weapons on Uhtred and his men, with their bowstrings drawn and the iron tipped arrows ready to let fly.

I held tight to Rinan's cloak, and peering over the spiked tops of the palisade, I was startled to see Eorl Uhtred gripping the reins of his warhorse and staring up at me. A long chain mail shirt protected his powerful body. The beaked nose and cheek guards of his helmet covered his beardless, battle scarred face, and he tilted back his head to look defiantly at our archers' goose-flighted arrows. Then lifting his sword, the blade flashed in the cold sunlight, and his black cloak billowed out behind him. He looked like a sea eagle, hovering with spread wings in search of prey, and it was good to be with my kinsmen on the walkway, and safe from the Eorl's sword arm.

'Look well, Godwin,' Uhtred shouted, his voice harsh above the tugging wind. 'The blood of your hearth lord Leof is on this blade. I

5

killed him in fair fight – his land is now mine. I am your new hearth lord. Open the gates and pay your taxes to me, if you have wit enough to accept my protection and save your people.'

My father stood firm footed on the platform, his head thrust forward, and his long straw-coloured hair tangling in the wind. Then throwing back his heavy woollen cloak from the bronze brooch at his shoulder he roared, 'What good is your protection? You'll take everything we have, you treacherous dog!' He pointed with his axe at the wolf's head in the rutted cart tracks. 'Uhtred – that's the only payment you and your kind will ever receive.'

The Eorl swivelled in the saddle, looking across the strips of land around our settlement, rich with peas, beans, cabbages, and winter corn, and across the heathland to the forested hills, teeming with game. Then he raised his voice above the heavy crump of the tide and the screaming gulls and shouted, 'I won this land in fair fight. Pay your taxes to me, Godwin, or die!'

'Never! You killed our hearth lord – he had no quarrel with you. He was a good man. You'll not stop your killing until all Northumbria is yours. You've slain Eorl Leof, so now we have no hearth lord but the king. We'll wait until King Aethelred comes from the border wars to swear our allegiance to him. We'll never bow knee to *you* as hearth lord!'

'The king, the king, the king,' my kinsmen chanted. Roaring their defiance, they stamped their feet so hard Rinan bounced into the air, bumped down on the walkway, and squealed with delight.

Uhtred shook his fist, his voice full of hatred. 'You'll regret your words, blacksmith. When I return I shall slaughter you, your family, and all your kinsmen.' Snatching at the reins, he wheeled his horse and dug his heels into its flanks. Then urging the piebald across the springing turf, he galloped away with his household bodyguards scattering after him across the heath.

Uhtred's threats ran round in my head as I watched the riders turn onto the coast road, and I felt relieved when they galloped south towards the king's great fortress at Bamburgh. I hated the look of it, darkly visible for many miles, perched high on a rocky outcrop at the edge of the wild North Sea. Feeling like a traitor, I was secretly wishing my father had taken Eorl Uhtred as hearth lord, for I was sure something terrible was going to happen to us all.

My kinsmen hurried down the ladders, shouting as if they'd won a famous victory. They were like proud men the minstrels sing about in winter tales. Men who marched into the king's hall, carrying gold rings and gilded armour they had stripped from the dead on the field of battle. Blood raced through their veins and it was only my father's thunderous voice brought them to their senses.

'There'll be time to celebrate with the wine cup when Uhtred is defeated,' he shouted, thrusting the shaft of his axe through his broad leather belt. 'The Eorl will return with many veteran huscarls, the fiercest of his warriors, not with a few of his household bodyguards. We must come quickly to the folk moot and decide what to do. It will be hard to defend the gates against his mercenaries.'

'The folk moot, the folk moot,' my kinsmen shouted, and hurried after father towards the meeting place, and the women stood in the doorways of the houses calling nervously to each other. Hearing their anxious voices made me worry about the people Uhtred had driven from their land. Would we be like them, living as outlaws, stealing from pigpens and sheepfolds, and attacking travellers on the road?

Helping Rinan to the bottom of the ladder, with these fearful thoughts in my head, I saw Heolstor, my father's brother, running across the yard with the ash spear in his hand. Heolstor was jealous of his brother, for my father had been Eorl Leof's faithful warrior, receiving many gifts from his lord on the battlefield.

This made me wonder what mischief Heolstor planned, and pulling Rinan by his cloak, I hurried with him to my hiding place beside the wall of my uncle's weaving shed. Here, half hidden by clumps of sea holly, I could listen to the men talking without them seeing me. Squatting down and hissing at my brother to be quiet, I watched them gather around the high stone cross and make way for Heolstor and the ash spear.

Men had carved the cross, patterned with winged beasts and birds with insect eyes, when the good Saint Cuthbert walked our roads, bringing the strange Christian message of kindness and love to our warrior people. It was a message my uncle Heolstor needed to hear, and I was wishing the saint alive today, to speak to my uncle about his jealousy and anger, when Rinan jumped up, tried to run to father, and I barely had time to snatch at his cloak and pull him back.

8

'Keep still, wriggly little eel,' I whispered angrily. 'If the men see us, we'll both be beaten.'

This quietened him, for he knew about beatings, and I settled to watch the members of the folk moot with a feeling of great bitterness in my heart. I was old enough to attend the meetings and join their war talk, but there was no place for me. With my useless leg, they would never send me into the forest to kill my first wolf and I would never be thought of as a man.

Many nights I dreamed I was searching for the wolf, only to wake sweating, shouting, and filled with sick fear. The creatures often hunted in packs and it would be dangerous work, but I longed for my chance to prove my worth. Boys of my age had slain the wolf and now sat by right at the meeting place and pitied me. Their pity did not upset me much, for it was kindly meant, but some like Oswold, uncle Heolstor's son, threw stones at me and shouted insults that made me burn with anger.

At my birth, my kinsfolk saw my bad leg and voted to leave me on the hillside for the wild beasts to eat, but father would not let them tear me from my mother's arms. He followed the teachings of the good Saint Cuthbert, and knew it wrong to kill a helpless child, and I was thinking it was a blessing to have such a father, when a sudden shout made me jump.

'Godwin, what use is your folk moot?' It was Heolstor, his face like thunder, spitting angry words, and threatening my father with the ash spear. 'There's no king's man to attend the meeting, no one to hold the spear and judge what should be done.'

My father growled and wrenched the spear from his brother's hand. An anxious cry went up, for the king's high reeve held the ash spear to decide right from wrong. Clenching the spear in his huge fist, as tough as the hammers he used to beat the glowing iron on his anvil, my father gave so threatening a look the men placed their weapons on the ground and squatted in the sand, waiting to hear him speak.

Only Heolstor and his friend the carpenter remained standing, both mean tempered and dangerous. 'Send for the king's high reeve,' the carpenter said, 'what gives you the right to hold the ash spear, Godwin?'

'I'm your chosen tythingman, head of this folk moot,' my father said, grim faced and hard voiced. 'We've old men who can judge more wisely than any reeve. While we wait for the king's man to come from Bamburgh, Eorl Uhtred will round up his cut-throats and be on his way to murder us.'

'I say give Uhtred what he wants – then he'll leave us in peace.' It was the potter, nervously twisting his clay stained hands, his thin face crumpled with fear. 'Better for us to be poor than be slain or outlawed!'

'Uhtred means to take all we have,' my father said. 'He'll not stop till he's destroyed every village in Northumbria. He'll leave us to face the coming blood month with no animals left to slaughter, and an empty grain pit, whether we accept him as hearth lord or not. What good are your clay vessels if we have no food to put in them potter?

10

We'll starve long before the weed months come. I say it's best to fight Uhtred now, rather than die a slow death from hunger, grubbing like wild boars in the snow filled forest.'

The men began to argue, each one standing in turn to shout his opinion and some agreeing with my father and others not. Then an elder kinsman, bent-backed and almost blind, struggled to his feet. Helped by those around him, he made his slow way to my father, who carefully closed the old man's hands around the spear.

Stooped and clinging to the shaft, the elder spoke, his scratching voice thin against the restless wind. 'Only King Aethelred–'

'Old man, you're a fool. King Aethelred is away, too busy fighting the border wars with Mercia to bother with us,' the carpenter mocked. 'No great lord at Bamburgh would protect the likes of you against Uhtred. They're traitors the lot of them. With the king gone they are Uhtred's men now, and obey his orders.'

'Our defences will hold for many days,' the elder said, fighting for breath. 'With the king no longer in Bamburgh, we must send a man to find him. Aethelred will return when he hears how his traitorous nephew destroys his villages, kills his thegns, and murders his people. I say we must choose someone to ride to the king and tell him of our danger. Eorl Uhtred must be punished for his crimes.'

Exhausted, he sank down amongst the thistles, and the spear fell from his hand. The men argued loudly with each other again, but my father Godwin roared at them, telling them time was wasting, and they must choose a man to go to Bamburgh.

11

Ignoring my father, my uncle picked up the spear, strutted like a cockerel, and ordered the young men to scour the ground for straw. They hurried to do his bidding, bringing their gleanings to him, and Heolstor roughly shook the elder, pulling him to his feet. Then counting the straws and pushing them into the frail man's hand, he beckoned my kinsmen to step forward, and I waited nervously to discover who would take the shortest straw.

TWO

Escape to the Forest

The men crowded round the old man, snatching at the straws, and it was hard to see what was happening. Then a gasp went up, the men fell silent, and I knew a man was chosen.

Those standing around the elder moved away and settled on the ground, and I went cold with fear, for my father was alone beside the cross with a wisp of straw between his large fingers and thumb.

'I would rather fight beside you to the death than ride to Bamburgh,' my father said, his voice loud and clear, 'but you see I cannot, for I hold the short straw. I know you will defend the settlement with your lives, but there is little time before Uhtred returns. First the women and children must be sent to safety in the forest.'

'There's no safety in the forest,' the carpenter sneered. 'The wolves and bears–'

'Bears? There are no bears left in the forest as well you know, carpenter. Better for the women and children to take a chance with wolves, than face Uhtred's mercenaries,' my father exclaimed.

'Godwin, it's not for you to decide these things. You will be safe in Bamburgh,' the carpenter mocked. 'Let those who must stand at the gates decide what is right! I say we choose Heolstor for tythingman.

He has the ash spear, let him decide.'

The men shouted so loudly it was impossible to hear what they said, until the weaver, red-faced with anger, jumped to his feet and tore the ash spear from Heolstor's hand.

'Godwin is right!' he yelled, poking Heolstor's belly with the tip of the weapon. 'Uhtred will be at our gates and we are fools, fighting over who shall be tythingman when our families are in great danger!' Then throwing the spear to the ground, he picked up his double-edged axe, ran across the yard, and called to his wife to collect food and clothing and run with the children to the forest.

This seemed to decide things for the others, and one by one, they gathered up their weapons and followed him, though some were arguing still. My father strode towards our house, and I lurched forward on my good leg, pulling Rinan after me. 'Let go, let go!' he shouted and tried to punch me, and I was spinning him round by his cloak when father called angrily for us to stop our fighting and waited until we caught up with him.

'I noticed you listening to the war talk, Toland, so you know I must be off to Bamburgh,' father said. 'You're not yet a man, but now I leave you to face a danger greater than any wolf and I'm sorry I did not think to make a sword to celebrate your coming of age.'

He glanced down at my bad leg, making me feel miserable. I needed no reminder I would never kill the wolf, and I was about to give an angry reply when he said gruffly, 'Take my hunting knife. Use it to defend your family, but never without just cause.'

14

Then he hung the knife, with its decorated leather case and metal hooks, from my belt, and I forgot my hurt and anger. Feeling like a warrior ready for battle, I shouted, 'I shall stay with my kinsmen and fight at the gates. I shan't go with the women to the forest, that's not men's work, I shall–'

'Enough. You'll have more than one man's work caring for your family, boy,' my father growled. 'You'll do as I say! You'll go with them and protect them with your life. Your foolish words make me think I leave them in the care of an idiot!'

My face burned with shame, and I could not look at him, but he gave a hard laugh and I felt his huge hand, like the paw of a bear, placed on my shoulder.

'No more senseless words, Toland,' he said. 'Go north through the forest. Get as far from Bamburgh as you can. Find the path we travelled last summer – it will bring you out of the forest not far from the crossing place to Lindisfarne where the monks live. Make sure there's no one on the coast road before you cross, and then follow the track to Elwick. Your mother's kinsman Siward will give you shelter.'

He gripped my shoulder so tight it made me wince. 'Uhtred will hunt you down, now I've stood against him. You must leave quickly – protect your family as I would myself!'

His words terrified me and my throat went dry, but I nodded, and he was about to stride away when he noticed Rinan staring up at him. My brother's mop of flaxen hair was sticky with food and coated with dust, and in his small fist he held a stalk of dried cow parsley for an ash spear, and he offered it to father.

'Rinan, do as Tolland tells you – obey him in all things,' father said and bent down to take the cow parsley from my brother's hand.

Rinan was not pleased to obey me, and muttered angrily, but he did not answer back, even if he'd dared, for father hurried towards the house and my brother trotted after him. By the time I reached home, father was speaking to my kindly mother at the door, and a jolt of panic went through me. He'd put on his chain mail shirt, the tunic decorated with Eorl Leof's twisted dragons, and he was ready for battle. His broad face with its big nose and bushy eyebrows looked fierce, and pulling on his heavy iron and bronze helmet, he walked to the shelter against the side of our house and led out the mare.

Patting her neck, she whinnied and nuzzled him, and he hung his long handled throwing axe from the saddlebag, threaded Rinan's cow parsley through his brooch clasp, and sprang into the creaking saddle. Then turning to look down at me for a moment, he gathered the reins and urged the mare forward.

I ran after him across the yard, but shouting for me to go back, he guided the mare across the rattling planks of the bridge. My uncle Heolstor rushed passed me holding the ash spear, and I heard him giving orders to the slaves as though he were already tythingman. This made me seethe with anger, and with a heavy heart, I watched my father until he reached the Bamburgh road and I could see him no more.

I'd been brave when father was there, but now self-pitying tears

16

threatened to spill down my face, and I angrily rubbed my eyes. Rinan hurried to me and nervously reached up to pat my hand, but I didn't want him to see me cry and I pushed him away and told him to follow me.

Inside the house, smoke from damp logs in the sandbox swirled around and made me cough, and through the gloom, I saw my lazy hound Bodo sprawled in the rushes and grandmother huddled on a bench before the fire. The goat lifted her head and bleated, hoping I'd give her stale cabbage stalks, and I worried what would happen to her when we were gone.

Mother was talking anxiously to herself as she shut the lid of the clothes chest and snatched up bread and cheese from the trestle table against the wall. Then quickly wrapping the food in cloths she pushed the bundles into her bulging reed basket and added a jug of her ale.

I was pleased to see the food and ale, and waited for her to tell me what to do, but she was looking at me in a strange way and I suddenly remembered father had left me to care for my family. A sick nervousness filled my belly and I tried to speak, but the words stuck in my throat. I swallowed hard and tried again, and this time the words came out in a terrible rush and I spluttered, 'Grandmother, you must come with me to the forest, Eorl Uhtred is on his way to attack us!'

To my dismay, grandmother took no notice of me and clung to the bench with swollen fingers. 'Let me be, I'm an old woman,' she muttered crossly. 'I'll not come with you.'

I didn't know what to do. I'd never given an order to my

grandmother in my life, afraid as I was of her quick temper and sharp tongue. I looked down at her, took a deep breath, and said, 'I'm not leaving without you, grandmother – if you stay to be killed – then I shall be killed too.'

This brought mother to nervous life, and pulling on her cloak, she called Rinan to her side and forced his feet into his boots. He fought to kick them off, and in the small amount of light coming through the open door, I could see mother's frightened face under her mantle. Then trying to make my voice sound like father, I said, 'Go quickly, mother, I'll follow with grandmother. Rinan, listen to me and stop being a baby. Take the path through the forest to the old hut where we found the mushrooms – wait for me there.'

Rinan took mother's hand and tugged, but she didn't move.

'Go, before Uhtred and his mercenaries return and kill you!' I shouted, and she fled from the house with Rinan clinging to her gown.

I bent down to grandmother at the hearth, and the familiar smell of wound-healing agrimony in the scrip at her waist was strong in my nostrils. Her old woollen cloak, stiff with wood smoke, hung loose about her shoulders, and careful not to hurt her thin neck, I fastened her saucer brooch.

She glowered at me from under strands of her rabbit's fur hair, her rheumy eyes as fierce as a she-wolf, and I backed away. Then thinking father would never forgive me if I left her there to die, I steadied my weight on my good leg and pulled her to her feet.

'Stop it, stop it,' she muttered. 'I hurt too much.'

18

'Uhtred and his men will break down the gates, I shall be murdered, and *you* will be to blame,' I shouted.

Hearing my unhappy voice, my dog Bodo stopped scratching fleas in his grey coat, sprang to his spindle legs, and came to snuff at my hand. The goat, sensing something wrong, bleated sadly, and I hurried to untie the creature, hoping she would not be evenmeat at the Eorl's table. Then calling my hound, I took a tight hold of grandmother's arm and led her from the house.

Bent and shrunken, she hardly reached my shoulder, and she shuffled so slowly I feared we would never reach the forest before Uhtred caught us. I longed to leave her and save myself, but I couldn't do it. I was desperate to make her walk faster, but she could only hobble at a snail's pace. Looking back, I saw the goat had followed us and was reaching up to the thatch above the door and eating it, and I was glad father wasn't there to see.

Men were running in the yard and cursing us to move out of their way, and one man yelled at Bodo and tried to kick him. Some of my kinsfolk were climbing ladders and passing weapons to those already on the walkway. My uncle Heolstor was at the gates, laughing to see us stumbling towards him, and did nothing to help his mother.

'Here he comes – old one leg. He's off to join the women in the forest where useless creatures like him belong,' he sneered at me. 'Come on, come on, old mother,' Heolstor shouted as grandmother. 'Move your old bones. I'm closing these gates – I can't wait forever. Be off with your cowardly grandson. He's running away to play hide-

and-seek in the forest and leaves the dangerous work to men.'

'Grandmother don't,' I whispered fiercely in her ear, for she was attempting to straighten her poor body, and I felt her quivering with anger. 'Keep going – say nothing to make him harm us – father will deal with him when he returns.'

I limped through the gates with grandmother struggling beside me, and I was thankful when we crossed the bridge and stood on the other side of the ditch. Then my heart sank when I looked along the stony track to the Edring Hills and saw the cold sun already beginning its slide towards the sea. It seemed such a distance to the forest. I longed to be back in bed and safe under the covers, not standing there in the tugging wind with Heolstor's crowing laughter loud in my head and the gates thudding shut behind me.

'We'll be all right, grandmother,' I said, but I was feeling more miserable than I'd ever been in my life before.

Then my lurcher pushed his damp nose into the palm of my hand, and looking down into his loving brown eyes, I was comforted. With Bodo beside me it wouldn't be so frightening, whatever happened.

THREE

Wolf Attack

'Good dog, good dog, Bodo,' I said, and the hound wagged his long thin tail against my legs. Then thinking he'd soon be coursing the wild brown hares, his body quivered with excitement.

The last of our women and children were hurrying up the track to the forest, and the sound of a little one's cries carried to me on the wind. 'It's not far, we'll soon catch up with the others,' I said, but in my heart I knew they would leave us far behind.

'Well, come on. What are you waiting for? Going to stand there till I'm froze to death?' grandmother grunted, pulling at my arm. 'Shan't need Uhtred to kill me. I'll be dead and stiff long before he gets here.'

The icy wind whipped strands of hair across her sooty, apple-wrinkled face, and I took a firmer hold of her stick-like arm and felt her body shaking. I tried to hurry her along, but this made her wince with pain. There was no sign of Uhtred, but mingled with my fear of him, something else was bothering me. Stupidly, I'd forgotten my cloak and I had only my woollen tunic and trousers against the bitter weather.

It took a long time to walk from the gates to the nearby pig keeper's shelter, and we were some way from the empty pigpens when grandmother let go of my arm and gasped, 'I've got to stop – I can't breathe.'

'You can't stop,' I said in despair. 'Uhtred is coming – we must keep going.'

'Then he'll have to catch me. He won't want an old woman like me, anyway. Lot of nonsense,' she panted.

'It isn't nonsense,' I said, but she flapped her hands to push me from her and nearly fell over.

It was no use shouting at her. She was too weak to go on, and she collapsed wearily on the path. I crouched by her side, listening to the wheezing sound in her chest and waiting anxiously for her to recover. It was dangerous to stay where we were, for men on horseback would see us easily, and I was wishing I could be like the hares and hide in a scrape, when I felt grandmother tap my arm.

Hollow-eyed and weary, she held out her hands to me, and I pulled her up. 'Not far now,' I said, 'you'll sleep safe and warm in Elwick this night.'

'Humph – want to sleep in my own bed. I've no use for Elwick,' she grunted.

'How do you know? You've never been to Elwick.'

She began to mutter again, and not listening to her grumbling, I suddenly felt the wind slacken. It had changed direction, and now it blew from the shore and brought with it a thick sea mist rolling across the heath. With the wind behind us, it pushed grandmother along, making her take little running steps, and her cloak lifted and I thought she would tumble like a dry leaf along the track.

'Hold tight, grandmother, or you'll be blown away,' I warned, hoping to make her laugh.

'Good thing if I'm blow away – less of a burden,' she growled.

The thickening mist swirled round us, blocking out the cold sunlight, and tiny water droplets trembled on the ends of her thin hair. She seemed so small and weak, and trying to make her feel better I said, 'We are safe, grandmother, Uhtred and his men will never find us now.'

She didn't answer, and in the drifting fog, I began to remember stories our minstrel told us when we gathered round the fire last winter. These were horrible tales about monsters rising up from the mere with bloodied claws, creeping across the heath, and killing the bravest warriors, and I was scared and looking for these terrifying creatures and it was hard to see where we were going.

The bushes jumped out at me from the gloom in a frightening way, and the blanket of fog deadened all sound. I was desperate to break the eerie silence and I cleared my throat and said, 'We must be close to the forest, it can't be much further now, grandmother.'

'Where's the ground and sky got to? I don't like this, let's go home,' she said, and tried to turn back. She stumbled and I seized hold of her before she fell. Although she was only skin and bone, the muscles in my arms and back ached from supporting her.

'You can't go home,' I said. 'You mustn't give up, we're nearly there.' She leaned heavily against me, and I was wondering nervously if we were still on the path, when I noticed something in the mist and hesitated, unsure of what I'd seen.

More thoughts of terrible monsters crowded into my head, and I stared into the blinding whiteness until my eyes hurt. To my horror, there was a grey shape coming through the fog towards me and I gasped with fear. Towering above me, it stretched out long arms. I backed away, tugging at grandmother and calling frantically for Bodo.

'Let go of me! You're hurting!' grandmother growled. 'Where are we going? Are we lost?'

I shook with fear. The horrible beast had stopped and was peering down at me, silently watching and waiting. I pulled grandmother one way, she pulled me another, and we stumbled round in circles. Bodo charged passed me, nearly knocking grandmother over, and raced towards the monster.

'Come back, Bodo,' I shrieked. 'Come back!'

I let go of grandmother and ran after him. The beast swooped towards me through the mist, but I didn't care, I had to save my dog. Screaming at Bodo to stop, I hurled myself at the monster, banged my head, and realised I was furiously punching the rough bark of a tree with twigs and acorns bouncing off me.

'Can't see what all the fuss is about,' grandmother said, sniffing indignantly as she stumbled passed me. 'Could have found the forest for myself without you pushing and shoving.'

Feeling foolish, and terribly afraid she would make fun of me for attacking a tree, I said defensively, 'It was *you* did the pushing - you didn't know which way to go.'

I took her arm and hurried her along faster than I should have done, making her cry out. She reached up and cuffed me, but I think it hurt her poor hand more than it hurt me. At least she didn't mention how scared I'd been and I was grateful to her for that.

It was much colder under the trees, there was a dank smell of earth mingled with the sharpness of rotting leaves, and I longed for my winter cloak. Voices echoed somewhere in the vast woodland and seemed to be calling to each other, and I hoped they were people from my settlement and not Uhtred's men coming after me. A squirrel scampered across the forest floor at my feet, making me jump. Bodo barked and chased after it, but it ran swiftly up the trunk of the nearest tree and chittered at him angrily from the safety of a branch.

'I'm freezing, let's go home,' grandmother said and tried to pull away from me, but I held onto her, pleading with her to keep going. Then with a shuddering sigh she set off again, and I was helping her through thick undergrowth when I thought I heard a deep baying a long way off in the forest and I stopped to listen.

Not many days before, I'd been with father coursing hares and seen Uhtred urging his mount across the heath into the forest, hunting wild boar with men and dogs. I'd forgotten Uhtred's vicious hunting pack. It wouldn't matter if the fog hid us or not, if he'd loosed the dogs they would sniff us out.

'Now what?' grandmother muttered. 'What are you stopping for?'

'Can't you hear it?'

'Hear what?'

The barking had ceased and although I waited, I didn't hear the sound again. I looked along the track through mist clinging like cobwebs to the trees and bushes. I was anxious and worn out from supporting grandmother, and I was uncertain which path to take.

'Humph — what's wrong with you? Don't you know the way?' grandmother said, digging me in the ribs with her bony elbow.

'I know the way, we can't be far from the hut,' I said angrily, rubbing my side.

'How do you know? Can't see my hand in front of my face.'

'Listen,' I said, so angry I didn't care if I frightened her. 'Didn't you hear? Didn't you hear the dogs?'

'What dogs? I'm not deaf.'

I listened again and heard grandmother fighting for breath, the soft patter of leaves drifting to the forest floor, and small creatures scuttling in the undergrowth. There was no more barking, but now I heard a faint trickling noise that filled me with sudden relief.

'I've found it!' I said excitedly, giving grandmother a hug.

'Get off me! Found what?'

'There. Can't you hear the stream?'

'Humph – thought we were looking for a hut.'

'The hut is near the stream, we're not lost after all.'

'Told you we were lost,' she said.

Trying to keep my temper, I led her towards the gurgling and chuckling sound that grew steadily louder and felt the first few spots of icy rain prickle my skin. Falling softly on the canopy of leaves it was slowly thinning the fog, and I recognised the place I visited last summer. Tall bushes were growing thickly on one side of the path and there was a muddy bank on the other.

At the bottom of the slope, water rushed noisily over pebbles and swirled round boulders, and there was Bodo, eagerly lapping with his long soft tongue, his thin flanks heaving from chasing squirrels. I called to him, and he scrambled up the bank to join me. Then running ahead, he played a game of stalking, jumping out like a ghost and vanishing again into the bushes. I scolded him, afraid he would get under grandmother's feet and trip her, and he flattened his ears, scampered off, and soon there was the sound of digging and the thwack of soil spattering the tree trunks.

Telling grandmother it wasn't much further, the track went deeper into the forest, and she grumbled, saying she wouldn't go another step and tried to sit down. I begged her not to stop, and struggling to keep her on her feet I saw an open space ahead where someone had felled many trees and shouted, 'Grandmother, we're here, we're here at last!'

Now long deserted, the cleared land was slowly returning to forest with hundreds of oak saplings growing through the leaf mould. There was an orchard of old apple trees, the fruit fallen and rotted, and in the middle of what had once been the garden was the charcoal burner's hut, its roof thatch fallen in at one end.

Anxiously looking for mother and Rinan, I said, 'Wait here, grandmother. I'll see if the hut is safe. Sometimes robbers use these places.'

'I'm not afraid of robbers,' she muttered, 'hurry up! I want to get out of this rain!' Finding a tree for shelter, she lowered herself awkwardly to the ground and seemed smaller than ever and drooping.

I heard Bodo nearby, busy with his own exploring, and I called him to me. He trotted up, his long snout covered with soil and eager to follow me, but I ordered him to stay with grandmother and the hound sat obediently at her feet and wagged his tail.

Climbing over what used to be the vegetable bed, with seeding cabbages blackened by the early frosts, I limped towards the silent hut. Seeing a hole where the door had once been, I peered inside, and in the soft grey light streaming through the fallen thatch, two white faces were staring up at me. Jumping back with a yell, I heard someone call my name, and recovering from my fright, I realised it was mother and Rinan sitting on a pile of straw.

'I thought you'd never find your way in this fog,' mother said anxiously, 'where's grandmother? What's happened to her?'

Before I could answer, Bodo rushed into the hut in a whirl of mud and leaves with grandmother stumbling slowly after him. 'I heard shouting,' she muttered, and pushing passed me flopped down on the straw.

'We can't stay here,' I said in alarm, watching her settle beside mother. 'We must find the path to take us to the coast.'

'Toland,' mother said in the tone of voice she used to Rinan when he wouldn't go to bed. 'We shall eat and drink first.'

'It's too dangerous, we *must* keep going. It's nearly dark and father told me–'

'Your father isn't here now. Even if he were he'd tell you grandmother must rest if she's ever to reach Elwick this night.'

'It is foolish to stay any longer,' I said, but mother spread a cloth on the straw, took bread, cheese, and the jug of thin ale from her basket, and wouldn't listen.

I was desperate to leave, and I was about to tell her I'd heard the dogs when I changed my mind. Mother was right, we wouldn't get far with grandmother so weak, and I decided not to scare her. Besides, there'd been no more barking since I first entered the forest and I was glad to stop for a while. My back and arms ached terribly from helping grandmother, and my bad leg was numb from dragging myself along.

'I suppose it won't do any harm to stay here for a few moments,' I said, sitting on the straw beside the others and quickly tearing at the crusty bread mother gave me. Then stuffing creamy goat's cheese into my mouth, I gulped down more than my share of ale. That made me feel better, and I was wiping my mouth with the back of my hand, and glancing around for Bodo to give him a scrap of bread, when fear gripped my belly.

'Where's Rinan?' I asked.

'He went after Bodo to give him a bit of cheese,' grandmother said.

'You should have stopped him! It's too dangerous for him to be alone in the forest,' I said wearily, and grabbing hold of one of the roof posts and hauling myself to my feet, I limped painfully from the hut.

The rain clouds had moved inland, clearing the fog, and I tramped through the wet garden in the dusk, calling my brother's name. He didn't answer, and I shouted for Bodo, thinking Rinan would be with him, but my hound did not come. Limping fast, my own tiredness now forgotten, I left the clearing and hurried along the track into the forest. Angry with Rinan for going off, I was desperate to find him.

Seeing bushes moving, I sighed with relief, but it was only my lurcher bounding towards me, and I patted him and said, 'Where's Rinan, Bodo? Good boy, where's Rinan?'

My hound trotted away, first making sure I was following, and led me back along the path to the stream, and from the top of the bank, I saw my brother crouched below me on the pebbles. He was busy placing twigs on the surface of the rushing water, watching them float away, and crowing with delight.

'Look, Toland,' Rinan said happily when he heard me call. 'Look at my twigs.'

'You mustn't go off on your own,' I scolded, 'come here.'

Reluctantly he left his game, slowly pulled himself up the bank, and I seized hold of him and shook him. Then dragging him along the path he squealed and tried to kick and bite me.

Struggling to quieten him, I shouted, 'Bodo, good boy, where are you Bodo?'

Annoyed at the dog for running off, I was calling him again when the bushes parted, and he was moving slowly towards me, but something was wrong. Bodo's legs seemed shorter, there were dark markings on his head and chest where none should be, and my throat closed in fear. It was a wolf.

FOUR

No One to Celebrate

The wolf was creeping along the ground, snarling and flattening its ears. I thrust Rinan behind me, unable to look away from those fierce yellow eyes and my chest so tight with fear I hardly breathed.

With trembling hands, I felt for father's hunting knife and dragged it from my belt. Why didn't the wolf attack? What was it waiting for? It was so close I could see every coarse hair on its forehead, the dark flecks in its eyes, and the softer hair along its ears. Its nose wrinkled and the black lips parted. Saliva dripped from its open mouth and it was bunching its hindquarters, ready to spring.

'Run, Rinan!' I yelled.

The beast leapt awkwardly towards me and I lurched sideways, landing heavily on my bad leg. It buckled under me and I slipped and tumbled down the bank, crashed onto the bed of the stream, and banged my head on a boulder.

The shock of icy water brought me to my senses, and I staggered to my feet. Frantic to save Rinan, I saw the wolf watching me from the path with its head lowered and it was holding up a front paw. The animal was injured! That's why its leap had been so clumsy, why it looked so thin. It was hurt – I had a chance to kill it! Snatching at the branch of a small sapling to begin the difficult climb up the bank I realised I'd dropped my knife!

Numb with fear, I looked desperately down at the water churning round my feet and tore at the swaying weeds. Plunging my hands into crevices between the rocks and seeing the watery outline of a knife resting on pebbles I made a grab for it. The blade cut deep into my fingers and a searing pain burned through my body. Shaking my head with shock, I managed to slot the knife back into its leather case.

Slowly dragging myself up the slope and trembling with exhaustion, I was almost at the top when I caught a glimpse of Rinan's white face peering at me from the bushes. The wolf was leaning over the edge of the bank, darting its head forward and trying to snatch at me with its teeth. Pulling myself up with one hand, and fumbling for my knife, I stabbed at its nose to frighten it and it backed away.

Still threatening it with my knife, I forced my tired body onto the path. Limping towards the growling animal, I thought it was going to turn and run, but it stood its ground. To my horror, it was balancing on three legs and gathering strength to leap. I gripped my knife, so terrified I didn't feel the pain in my cut fingers. The wolf hurled itself towards me and I wasn't quick enough to defend myself. It thudded into my chest, knocking me over, but before it could close for the kill Bodo tore like a whirlwind from the bushes, thumped into the wolf's side, and sent it sprawling.

It scrambled back onto its feet, snarling and ready to attack. The two animals collided with a clash of teeth, and jaw-to-jaw in furious combat they flung each other about, spinning in a storm of leaves, twigs, and mud. Bodo was taller but made for speed not strength, and although the wolf was hurt, the muscles of its broad shoulders and chest were still strong, and it fought savagely for its life. Breaking free from my hound's grip, it buried its teeth in his neck. Bodo screamed and hurled the wolf from him. It slid along the path and turned to attack again.

They fought in a growling, heaving mass of fur, feet scrabbling in the dirt and locked together to the death. Bodo was weakening. If I didn't do something to help him, my hound would die. With a cry of rage, I staggered to my feet with my knife raised. My lurcher was on the ground, the wolf's jaws deep in his side, and I struck, sinking the blade into the wolf's back. Crying with fear and anger, I stabbed and stabbed, tears pouring down my face. The wolf gave a terrible moan and I watched in horror as it took a few steps, dragged its body away from me, and collapsed and died.

I stumbled about, waving my knife and yelling I'd killed my first wolf. Wild with terrible excitement, I laughed and cried, my heart hammering in my chest. I longed for father to be with me, but there was no one to celebrate my manhood, and looking round for Rinan and Bodo, I saw my poor hound lying twisted on the path.

Throwing myself beside him, there was no sight in his eyes and his tongue was hanging from his mouth. Rinan ran from his hiding place and put his arms round Bodo's torn neck, and there was a great gash in my dog's side where the wolf's fangs had ripped him open.

34

'Get up, Bodo,' Rinan said, giving him a shake. 'Get up, Bodo! Why won't he get up, Toland?'

'Rinan,' I said angrily, pulling him off Bodo's body. 'If you hadn't left the hut Bodo would not have died. See what your foolishness has done!'

'Why won't Bodo get up?' my brother wailed.

I tried to think what to do. I didn't want to leave my hound there on the path, but we had to hurry. If my father was right, it wouldn't be long before Uhtred came looking for us. Giving my lurcher's silky domed head one last stroke, my tears soaking his soft fur, I limped back along the path to the hut, leaving Bodo alone and my brother trailing miserably behind me.

Mother jumped up from the straw with a shriek when she saw Rinan with blood on him, and I said quickly, 'It's all right, it is Bodo's blood – my hound died helping me kill the wolf.'

'Bodo is dead?' she gasped and I nodded, so upset I didn't want to talk about it, and she gave me a hug. 'Bodo was a good and loving friend. I'm sure Saint Cuthbert will take care of him,' she said.

'Why should he care for a dog?' I muttered. 'We must hurry. We've stayed too long – we must find the path to Elwick.'

She nodded, but then she cried out in horror to see blood dripping from my fingers. Grandmother called me to her, opening her scrip and stuffing soothing agrimony leaves into the cuts, and mother fussed around me, binding my hand with cloth torn from her mantle. Then it was wonderful to see her pulling my winter cloak from her basket, and wrapping it round me, she was hurriedly fastening the brooch when I heard barking again in the forest.

I looked at mother in dismay. I could tell by her face that she'd guessed it was Uhtred's hunting pack, but we were both too scared to say anything. The barking was horribly close, and trying not to show my fear, I helped grandmother to her feet and hurried my family into the garden.

The frightening sound of yelping dogs was coming closer, and looking frantically around in the fading light at the dark clumps of bushes I said, 'There's a path–'

'Hurry up, boy,' grandmother grunted, swaying with exhaustion and her wisps of rabbit hair standing up on her head. 'There's a path or there isn't one!'

'I'll find it! I'll find it!' I said angrily, and I lurched forward, shouting to mother to help me search. Rinan ran after me, getting in my way, and I pushed him hard. He fell backwards into the bushes, and worried in case I'd hurt him, I found him lying on a stony path, partly overgrown with weeds.

'It's here,' I shouted. Roughly lifting my brother to his feet and telling mother to run with Rinan to safety, I seized hold of grandmother's arm and pulled her after me.

The path through the bushes went steadily downhill into trees so close together they made a narrow, winding tunnel. Not much light came through the tightly woven branches, and despairing at the slow steps grandmother took I was alarmed and angry to see mother and

Rinan hurrying back up the slope towards me.

'Keep going, save yourself and Rinan!' I said, pushing mother away, but she put her hand under grandmother's elbow and wouldn't let go.

'Slow down, slow down, you're hurting me,' grandmother groaned, her feet scraped and bruised as we dragged her along, but hearing excited barking echoing down the tunnel, we pulled her faster still.

Grandmother cried out in pain. The pack was gaining on us, and struggling for breath I panted, 'It's no use, the dogs are not far behind, keep going, mother. I'll stop them if I can. Keep going!'

Freeing myself from her clutching fingers, and ignoring Rinan's cries for me to stay, I turned and limped back up the hill. Now that I must face Uhtred's hunting pack, every bit of my body was alive and ready to do battle, and excitement took the place of fear. Clutching my knife in my stinging hand, I knew the attacking hounds were always reluctant to leave their kill. This would give my family more time to reach the coast. If I gave my life to protect them, father would be proud of me, and the only thing I longed for was to have dear Bodo by my side.

Soon I would come face to face with the racing animals, and with my knife held ready, I was startled to hear a soft growling. In the light filtering through the branches, I could see a strange looking hound settling its haunches on the path in front of me. It seemed to be waiting for Uhtred's dogs and a deep rumbling was coming from its throat.

Moments later, the first of the pack tore down the hill, baying and wild for the kill. I was ready to fight as long as I could, but to my astonishment, the charging hounds saw the dog crouched on the path at my feet and skidded to a halt, the fur on their backs rising. Screaming with fear, they tried to turn in the narrow space, colliding, snarling, and desperate to escape.

More and more hounds raced down the slope, sliding and climbing over each other and yelping in fright, and I stared in amazement at the biting dogs. A few of the strongest animals forced their way through the struggling bodies, scampering back up the hill, and the others scrambled after them, their tails between their legs.

Stunned by what had happened, I heard the shouts of men running through the forest after the howling dogs. Then noticing the strange hound had turned to look at me, I thought for a moment it might attack, but it slunk quietly through the trees and was gone.

Trembling with shock, I plunged down the path, slipping in the leaves. Not caring about branches whipping painfully against me, I didn't stop until I reached the bottom of the hill and stumbled from the trees. Gasping for breath, and unable to believe the dogs were gone, I saw the moon making a glittering path across the sea and heard the distant pounding of waves on the shore.

Mother was standing on the heath and looking anxiously towards the forest, her face as pale as the moon, and grandmother was slumped on the ground with Rinan curled up beside her fast asleep. I limped towards them and mother gave a cry when she saw me and hugged me so tight I couldn't breathe.

'You should have kept going,' I said angrily when she released me, 'why did you stop? You are almost at Elwick. You can see the village over there.' I pointed across the coast road to the thatched roofs, silver and black in the moonlight. 'You must hurry before the dogs come back!'

Without a word, and looking offended at my scolding, mother helped me lift grandmother to her feet. She moaned and said her body hurt so much she would sleep there for the night, but we didn't listen. Then mother picked up Rinan and carried him, and I took the weight of grandmother as she staggered beside me.

'How did you escape from the dogs?' mother said at last after we'd stumbled over the heath for some time in silence, her arms heavy with the sleeping Rinan. 'I couldn't go on without you.'

'There's no time to talk now,' I said. I was still angry with her for stopping on the heath, and I wasn't sure how I'd escaped because it had happened so quickly and mysteriously. Besides, I had other things to worry about. Grandmother was grumbling at every step and insisting she could go no further.

'We've come this far together, don't give up now, we're nearly there,' I said to her as patiently as I could. Holding tight to her arm I was telling her how brave she was when I heard more barking coming from the depths of the forest and shuddered.

Grandmother turned to look towards the trees and I knew she'd heard the noise. 'Humph! Don't like dogs – Bodo's all right,' she muttered, and began to walk almost as quickly as mother who carried Rinan in her arms.

There was a slight rise to the Bamburgh road, a silver arrow in the moonlight, dividing the heath and black forested hills from the villages along the coast. Leaving grandmother, I hurried up the slope, and seeing no one about, helped her to cross. Mother followed as best she could with her awkward burden, and it wasn't long before I found the stony track to Elwick through rough sandy pasture.

It was difficult to wade waist high through the thistle heads and grasses and keep grandmother from falling, but at every step, I could see the village coming closer. The thundering of the sea and the pebbles rolling and clattering on the shore grew louder, and the long grasses gave way to reed beds and flat salt marshes. The land was criss-crossed with drainage ditches and I had to take care grandmother didn't topple into them, but now I could see lights shining from the dark huddle of Elwick village and that gave me strength to go on.

There were no earthworks or palisade at Elwick, just a fence surrounding the wooden walls of the thatched buildings, silvery blue in the moonlight. Ahead was a pebbled path between the houses with smoke drifting through the thatch. Passing the sweet-sour stench of the piggeries and the stink of the cesspit, there was now the smell of cooking fish and onions.

Thoughts of safety and warmth, with maybe a little food, made us hurry the last few steps despite our weariness. With our footsteps crunching the path, we walked through deep shadows where house walls shut out the moonlight, and it was difficult to know one home from another. Mother kept saying she knew the way and then shook her head and said she was mistaken, and I wandered after her with grandmother's weight burning my arm.

I wanted to shout at mother to hurry up, and I was thinking we'd never find shelter that night, when at last she said, 'There – I'm sure,' and pointed to one house close to the shore, not far from where we stood. 'I'm certain that is Siward's home. Go and knock Toland – see if he will take pity and welcome us in.'

'Stay still, grandmother,' I said, 'I'll soon be back,' and I limped through the shadows to where a dull light shone through gaps in the oiled skins, and thumped with my fist on the door.

FIVE

In the Rubbish Pit

No one came for a long time. I waited, fearing that mother was mistaken and we'd come to the wrong house, or perhaps her kinsman no longer lived in Elwick.

Then I heard feet shuffling and my uncle's nervous voice crying, 'Who is it?'

'It is your kinswoman, Godwin's wife, with her children and Godwin's mother. She needs shelter for the night,' I shouted.

I heard the rattle of the wooden bar lifted, the door creaked open, and my uncle Siward peered into the shadows. Anxious to see who was there, he ducked his grizzled head beneath the thatch above the door and hopped onto the path.

'Is it Toland? What has happened?' he said, his old voice full of concern. Then he saw mother holding the sleeping Rinan, grandmother swaying and about to fall, and he hurriedly took her arm and led her into the house.

I followed mother, and my aunt Eacnung greeted her, making anxious noises and saying, 'Come in quickly - what has brought you here on such a cold night? You are all worn out!'

She pulled up a bench close to the fire and mother sat beside grandmother with Rinan in her lap. I waited, but no one said anything

42

to me, so I settled in the reeds, and in the flickering light from the burning rushes in the wall brackets looked around.

It was good with the fire burning brightly in the sand box, and I sniffed hungrily at the wonderful smell coming from the blackened pot hanging above the burning logs. My uncle Siward was fumbling to bar the door, shutting out the cold wind from the sea, and Eacnung, Siward's wife, plump like our hens and kindly, bustled about, bringing beakers of warmed apple wine for us to drink.

Mother shook Rinan and gave him some wine to sip, but he coughed, spluttered, slipped to the floor like a warm puppy, and was soon asleep in the reeds beside me. I found the liquid sharp and wonderful, and hearing mother thank my aunt for her kindness, I did the same. Listening to Siward's gruff questions, and mother's anxious replies, I thought about the happenings of the day.

Suddenly remembering the wolf I said, 'Uncle, I'm now a man! Today I killed my first wolf with the help of my hound. There was no one to celebrate, and my hound died saving Rinan and me. Only my brother was at the killing and he is a poor witness, for he is fast asleep.'

My uncle Siward nodded and patted me on the shoulder. 'I'm sure you tell the truth, boy, for why should you tell a lie about the brave dog who gave his life for yours? There will be celebration enough once you are home safe and the villain Uhtred is no longer destroying our villages.'

Pleased with his answer, I listened to the wind howling from the sea and thought of the wolf and my terrible encounter with it on the path. In my mind, I could see the creature, injured and hungry, and I wondered if Saint Cuthbert knew and cared about ravenous wolves that killed people to survive.

The wind buffeted the walls and tore angrily at the thatch, and I moved closer to the fire. I must have fallen asleep, for I woke with a start and heard Siward calling me to help with the trestle table and to pull up the benches. Then seated at table, Eacnung gave us thick slices of coarse bread and ladled fish stew into wooden bowls.

We'd not eaten much all day, and I gobbled the stew, digging my spoon deep to get at the bits of fish and burning my mouth. My brother woke up and ate a little of the stew, and I was about to say the food was very welcome when Siward put his finger to his lips and hushed me, and we sat very still, staring at the door.

'What is it?' I asked nervously.

'For a moment I thought I heard horses on the road,' he said, shaking his head. 'Uhtred has increased his attacks on villages these last days. He destroys settlements when they refuse to pay his taxes, but it's more than a desire for taxes is bothering him, I'll be thinking. He's like a tormented animal, crossing often to Lindisfarne to question the holy men. He searches for something, and I hope he finds it quickly and leaves us in peace. He grows more violent as each day passes. He'll never leave us alone till he finds what he's looking for – whatever it may be!'

'Why doesn't King Aethelred put an end to Uhtred's killings?' I said.

'The king knows nothing of his nephew's evil ways. Aethelred's away at the border wars with Mercia. While he's gone, the Eorl gathers more and more powerful men about him. Some say Uhtred has killed the king and intends to take Northumbria for himself.' He laughed bitterly. 'If he's not stopped, no one will be left to work his fields, tend his woods, or pay his taxes. There'll be deserted villages and none to do his bidding.'

'I fear he has attacked our settlement,' said mother sadly, 'with Godwin away–'

'We knew it was coming,' Siward said darkly. 'There have been warnings – strange sights at sea – signs of something terrible to come. Dreadful warnings appearing over this land, terrifying the people. We've seen lights rushing through the air, and there's talk of fiery dragons coming across the sea.'

'Husband, you talk too much and worry our kinsfolk,' said Eacnung, shaking her head. 'They're tired – they don't want to listen to stories to frighten children. We hear horses on the Bamburgh road many nights, and no one comes. I'll fetch fresh bedding, and–'

'There – will you listen, woman,' Siward demanded.

He was right, for I heard horses trotting down the pebbled track towards the village and loud barking. Uhtred and his hunting pack had sniffed us out.

'Quick, Toland,' said Siward, 'the table.'

I struggled to help him move the table and benches, and Eacnung

45

seized the cooking pot, sprinkled the remains of the fish stew over the floor, and hid the bowls. Siward scraped aside reeds littered with food scraps, lifted some planks, and beneath were three steps into a shallow pit.

'Go down,' Siward urged. 'This place is useful in such dangerous times.'

Falling over each other in our haste, we climbed down onto damp earth under the house. Mother helped grandmother who shouted she would stay where she was, and wanted no dark hole to sleep in, and I lowered the sleepy Rinan down and followed after. There was little room and we had to lie on the cold packed earth in scraps of rotted meat and fish bones that had fallen through gaps in the floor. It was even worse when my uncle and his wife dragged the boards shut over our heads.

The smell was disgusting and the slimy rubbish was crawling with insects. I thought I heard rats scuttling, and in the poor light coming through the floorboards, I saw mother with her cloak pressed over her mouth and nose. Grandmother shouted at mother, scolding her for being weak and stupid and for saying she felt sick, and mother tried to hush her.

Listening to the faint pattering of unseen creatures, I thought I heard a soft bark and wished I had Bodo with me, for he'd been a good ratter. Longing for my hound by my side, I felt a soft warm tongue lick my face, and telling myself to stop imagining things, the thought of him was comforting.

I lay there, listening to the sound of Siward's shuffling feet, and something gentle falling on the floor above me, and decided my uncle must be hiding the entrance to the pit with more reeds. Then it went quiet, and hoping the horses had ridden by and we were safe, I heard whinnying and a winded horse blowing through its nostrils close to the wall of the house.

Harnesses chinked as riders dismounted, feet crunched the pebbles. Excited hounds whined and barked, and someone shouted, 'Open up or we'll break down the doors!'

My brother woke up and whimpered. I whispered to him not to make a sound or we would die, and a thunderous banging on my kinsman's door drowned my anxious warning.

'Peace now,' Siward growled, 'I'm coming, I'm coming.'

Hearing a thump on the floor above my head, I guessed Eacnung had placed her stool over the entrance to the pit. Then the door crashed open and I heard Uhtred's cruel voice shouting, 'Where's Godwin's worthless whelp? You're kinsman to the misbegotten creature. Where is he? I'm told he came this way with others of his blood. Tell me where he is and you'll have three silver pennies – if you don't, I'll hang you and the old woman beside you!'

Three silver pennies! I wasn't sure how much that was, but I thought it must be enough for Siward to buy many chickens or a cow. Even if this wealth didn't tempt him, I knew my uncle would never let his wife die for the sake of kinsfolk who seldom came to visit, and I trembled and dreaded his answer.

'I've not seen my kinsman Godwin or his family for many months,' I heard my uncle say. His old voice was loud and defiant, and I breathed a sigh of relief mingled with hot shame, for I'd thought he would betray us.

Uhtred cursed and Siward cried out. I heard a heavy thud and Eacnung screaming and thought my uncle dead. Men were tramping about, and a horrible crashing came from above and the sound of tearing. Grandmother started an angry muttering and tried to sit up, and mother reached out to quieten her.

Dogs were darting about and sniffing, their feet pattering on the floor, their noses snuffling, but the stench of rubbish, mixed with the fish stew, must have hidden the smell of our bodies. They did not bark or scratch in the reeds to find us, and it wasn't long before an angry voice called them from the house and Uhtred cursed and shouted orders to search the village.

The door slammed so violently it creaked and banged on its hinges for a terrible time. I lay still, listening fearfully to the distant shouting and a horrible thought occurred to me. How did Uhtred know my family was with me? Would Heolstor have betrayed his own mother?

These terrible questions chased round and round in my head. Rinan was crying, mother was hushing him, but the shouting and barking went on for a long time. I felt an insect crawling over my face and brushed it off, and lying cold and cramped on the damp earth in that terrible stink I was frightened Uhtred's men would return and search for us again.

SIX

High Tide at the Crossing Place

There were heavy footsteps coming along the path and I heard men talking not far from the house. I held my breath, trembling at the thought of them so close to our hiding place and imagined them ripping up the floorboards and dragging us out.

Then to my enormous relief I heard them remounting and calling to the dog pack, and after a while, the sound of horses galloping along the coast road faded into the distance. A silence descended upon the village, broken only by the chattering pebbles with the lapping tide, wind tugging at the thatch, and a child crying.

It seemed a long time before Siward's wife lifted the planks and we crawled from that horrible pit into what was left of the house. Bed hangings were torn down, a chest broken, and benches smashed. Eacnung's loom was destroyed, and mother gasped in terror when she saw our kinsman Siward lying by the door with a bloodied head.

'He told Uhtred nothing, so they hit him. He fell and lost his senses and they left him for dead. Don't worry, his head's like iron, he's taken worse knocks than this,' Eacnung said with a grimace. She picked up a jug and tipped water over her husband who groaned and moved his legs. 'He came round a bit ago, but I told him to lie there until they'd gone. I'm glad he told them nothing. What would we want with three silver pennies in our old age?' she said bitterly.

Mother helped her lift Siward with his back against the door, and Eacnung said, 'They've gone north, you're safe for now, but you can't stay long. When Uhtred discovers you're not at the next village, or the next, he'll be back with a worse temper than before. He knows you are somewhere near and he'll search until he finds you.'

'Where can we go?' asked mother, brushing the scraps of food from Rinan's cloak, pulling a cabbage leaf from grandmother's wispy hair, and tears running silently down her tired and dirty face.

'There is a small house at Ancroft where a few nuns live - belongs to the mother church at Whitby. They'll protect you,' Eacnung said, and bent down to wipe blood from her husband's head with the hem of her gown. 'The nuns take pity on those who suffer from Uhtred's evil ways.'

'I'm tired and I smell so foul, Eacnung,' mother said wearily, 'and how can I find the nuns' house when I don't know the way?'

Siward opened his eyes and lifted his head to look at her. 'I'll go with you – the nuns know me and–'

'You're not fit to walk,' Eacnung protested, but Siward growled to silence her.

'I'm better now, don't fuss woman – see if your neighbours are safe,' he said, struggling for breath.

Grumbling to herself, Eacnung wrapped a shawl about her shoulders and left the house, and Siward refused mother's help and pulled himself unsteadily to his feet.

50

'First we must decide what to do about this growing son of yours,' he gasped, straightening his old back and swaying a little. 'If you go to Ancroft the nuns speak at the door – allow no man to enter.' He took a deep breath and leaned against the wall. 'They'll not mind a child like Rinan, but I shall find Toland one of Eacnung's old cloaks and a gown, then they'll think–'

'No,' I said indignantly, 'I'll have none of it. We're not far from Lindisfarne. I'll cross to the island and ask the monks for shelter. Father says they are good men who do no harm. I shall go to their monastery. I have seen them travelling along these roads and they may have news of my father.'

'If you intend to cross to the island then you must be quick,' Siward warned, sinking down onto a stool. 'It will soon be dawn – high tide is nearly upon us. I fear you'll be too late, and the Eorl will have left riders to hunt along the road while he searches the villages.'

'They'll not see me, I'll take care,' I said, feeling for the hilt of my knife. 'I'll hide in the dunes should I meet them on the road.'

'No, Tolland, if Uhtred's men don't catch you, the sea will carry you to your death,' mother said fearfully, 'and I'm frightened that the dogs–'

'Don't be, mother. We stink so horribly I'm sure no dog will nose us out.' I grinned at her, hiding my fear. 'I'll be safe on the island, father will return with the king, and we'll be rid of Uhtred for ever.'

My mother smiled through her tears and I was brave for her, and I was wondering if we would ever see father again when Eacnung

51

returned with news that all was well. Then hurrying about, she gave us water to wash, helped us brush the mess from our clothes, and when we were ready to leave, Rinan was awake and grandmother appeared more rested.

Grim faced and unsteady on his feet, Siward cautiously opened the door and in the pale light of dawn birds rose from the dunes. We stepped out into the quiet village and the sweep of sky turned slowly from soft grey to the palest blue, streaked with thin cloud. The dark fortress of Bamburgh on the outcrop near the shore grew clearer in the better light, and on its seaward side, I noticed the horrifying drop down the cliff face to the boulder-strewn beach.

Moving slowly through the rushes, Siward insisted on helping grandmother, and supporting her between us, we left the salt marshes behind and came again to the Bamburgh road. Then beckoning to mother and calling softly, Siward said, 'It's safe for now, but you must be quick and say your farewells. It's dangerous in the open with the light growing stronger.'

Mother hugged me as though she would never let me go. Grandmother reached up to touch my cheek and Rinan rushed at me, flinging his arms around my legs, and I ruffled his hair. Mother pulled him away and I watched them cross the road and walk along the lane to Ancroft, and I waited until a clump of trees finally hid them from view.

Making sure there was no one on the road, and feeling suddenly very lonely, I limped as fast as I could towards the north and the

Lindisfarne crossing place. It was a long exhausting walk, and I kept close to dunes along the margin of the bay. With my head down against the wind, I didn't hear the two horsemen until they appeared above the rise in the road and were coming fast towards me.

They were horribly close, and throwing myself belly down, I crawled frantically into the sand hills, terrified and hoping they hadn't seen me. Grasping handfuls of marram grass, my cut fingers stinging, I dragged myself into a hollow between two dunes and lay there, trembling all over. The sound of the trotting horses came closer, and expecting the men would seize me and drag me away, I curled up tight, choking with fear and my heart thudding.

The beating hooves were loud in my head, and I held my breath and waited, but nothing happened. To my enormous relief, the horses cantered passed, and with a long shuddering sigh, I listened to the sound of them moving down the road.

Exhausted and hardly believing the men were gone, I stayed still for a long time, and then very cautiously I struggled to my feet. Afraid to return to the road, I set off through the sand hills, but it was difficult with my feet sinking deep in the wind swept dunes. Weary, and my leg aching, I was glad to reach the damp, hard-packed sand of the bay and saw the island of Lindisfarne at last.

The crossing place was a long narrow road made from a pile of rocks with stakes driven deep in the sand to show the way. Excited that I might soon be safe, I hurried towards it. It didn't seem far, and I limped as fast as I could, but with growing alarm I realised the tide was moving swift in silent ripples towards me. It was coming from many directions, each dark sheet of water criss-crossing another and going to trap me. I backed away, but the rapidly advancing tide surrounded me, rising above my ankles and filling my boots.

The speed of the water was frightening. It was already up to my waist, and I fought to escape its powerful tugging. I turned and found I was far out in the bay and visible from the road. Starting to wade back towards the dunes as fast as I could, the sea slowed me down, and I hadn't gone far when I heard a shout.

A small group of horses had stopped on the road. One rider was galloping across the beach towards me, clumps of sand flying from his mount's hooves. The sucking tide was almost up to my shoulders. Men were shouting and pointing in my direction. The first rider urged his horse chest high into the water, but before he could reach me, a wave knocked me off my feet and carried me out to sea.

I let out a cry of fear, salt water slopped into my mouth, and powerful currents took me further down the coast. My woollen cloak was soaked, wrapping round me and pulling me down. I thrashed about, desperate to find sand under my feet, but I was out of my depth and sinking.

Kicking hard, I fought to keep my head above water. I'm a strong swimmer, but not strong enough to fight the weight of my wet clothes and the power of the tide. Carried further down the coast, I struggled to free myself from my cloak, but my brooch pin bent and it wouldn't come open.

Growing weaker, I saw white flecks of foam where waves were breaking over rocks. If I could swim that far, I might be able to cling to them until the tide retreated. Dragging the weight of my cloak behind me, I tried to swim but it was hopeless, and I sank beneath the waves.

SEVEN

The Hermit on Inner Farne

The sea closed over my head and I made one last despairing effort to reach the surface. Lifting my arms, and fighting the folds of my cloak, I kicked frantically with my one good leg.

I rose slowly to the surface, my lungs bursting, and moving patterns of light rushed towards me. I felt the weak sun on my face as seawater poured from me. Gasping for air, my arm struck something hard, and I felt my wrist seized. Strong hands grabbed the back of my cloak and pulled me spluttering and choking from the sea.

Coughing and wedged upside down in the bottom of a boat like a stranded fish, I heard an urgent voice shout, 'Keep still, you'll send us both to the bottom, you fool.'

Pressed against the thin wooden strips lining the hull, I feared the craft might capsize, and slowly turning onto my back, I found I was in a coracle, but it was not like any I'd seen on our meres and rivers. This was much larger and built for sea travel, and I sensed with good handling it would survive all but the roughest weather. Holding the gunwale I carefully pulled myself up and saw the first of the smaller islands, the one my kinsmen call Inner Farne, coming near, and the island of Lindisfarne growing smaller in the distance.

To my surprise, it was a girl sitting on the cross bench, paddling though the rolling waves. I watched her steer the boat with strong sure movements, her shoulders broad, and her arms thick and muscular. She was dressed like a boy, with tunic and trousers, both dark with sea spray, and her hair hung in a thick plait to her waist, the colour of a raven's wing.

I was envious of the way she handled the craft as it rose up the steep side of a wave and slid rapidly down the next, and I watched how skilfully she brought us to the cliffs of Inner Farne, rising sheer above us. Noisy sea birds wheeled and dived, and the cold sunlight glittered on the surface of the water. Seals swam lazily towards us, lifting their silky heads above the waves, and I was near enough to see their large dark shining eyes, thick fleshy nostrils, and their long stiff whiskers. They stared at me curiously, and the girl called to them with barking sounds and they answered her as they followed the boat.

Watching the seals, I suddenly noticed she was steering the coracle towards the cliff wall, and alarmed, and thinking we were coming too close and would be smashed to pieces, I shouted, 'Take care!' My heart raced with fear, but she shook her head, her plait bouncing in the wind, and I saw a narrow space between two headlands. Water was crashing and pounding against the foot of the cliffs, forcing its way into the gap, and the next powerful surge picked up the coracle and swept it into the channel.

I clung to the sides of the craft, expecting the rushing torrent to hurl us against the rocks, but fighting with her paddle she kept us clear of the walls towering above us, and carried forward at a terrifying speed she brought us safely to the end of the long passageway. Then the level of the water dropped and we glided into a small bay where the sea had carved a deep bowl into the cliffs. Overhead was a circle of blue sky filled with screeching gulls, and we were heading for a small shingle beach.

'Get ready to jump,' the girl said, and I gripped the sides of the coracle, pain shooting through my cut fingers, and braced myself.

The bottom of the boat jarred on pebbles and nearly flung me out, but managing to steady myself, I slid over the gunwale and fell into the sea. The water came up to my waist, and I stumbled forward, my feet sinking into shingle.

Wading onto the beach, I turned and was alarmed to see the girl already far from the shore. I called, but she didn't look back and a wall of water came pouring through the channel towards her. She waited until the speed of it slackened and swirled around the coracle. Then paddling furiously as the retreating tide sucked the boat into the gap between the cliffs, she disappeared from sight.

I was alone with only the gulls for company. I'd lost the cloth mother had wrapped round my fingers, and although the cuts still throbbed, the seawater had cleaned them. Not knowing what to do, I limped along the shore, hoping to keep warm.

I was worrying in case the girl had left me there to die, but why should she do that when she'd saved me from drowning? The feel of my icy clothing was horrible and my teeth were chattering. Thinking I'd freeze to death if she didn't come back, I was giving up hope of ever finding a way off the beach when I saw steps cut into the cliff.

Anxious to discover if there was someone on the island to help me, I tried to ignore the pain in my leg and climbed steadily, dragging myself higher and higher. Reaching the top of the cliff, the full force of the wind whipped round me, chilling me to the bone, and looking across the dark restless sea, I saw small islands strung out along the coast. Waves were fiercely pounding the rocks below me, and I was desperate to find shelter. Then noticing a narrow well-trodden path, and following it to a rocky outcrop, I squeezed between huge boulders carved into strange shapes by the fierce storms, and found a quiet grassy space sheltered from the wind.

Within the rough circle of protecting rock, there was a hut built of closely fitting stones, the shape of a beehive. I hurried around it, but finding no window place or door, discovered a low arched entrance into a long narrow tunnel. Ducking my head, I limped along the dark passageway and nearly fell down a short flight of steps onto a floor cut into the rock and covered with reeds.

On a stone hearth was a fire of crackling driftwood, and in the leaping glow from the burning wood, I saw a small hand mill, a half finished piece of weaving made from coarse sheep wool hanging on a loom weighted with stones, and a chest. A table stood against the curving wall with a cross on it, but it was not like the one at the folk moot. It was small and simple and made from wood, smoothed and polished by the sea.

There was a pile of reeds covered with goatskins, and too tired to care what might happen if the owner of these things returned, I threw off my wet clothes and spread them to dry before the fire. Then kicking off my boots, I pulled the warm animal skins over me, snuggled into the reeds, and fell into a disturbed sleep.

Horrible dreams came to torment me, and I was in the forest with Uhtred's dogs racing towards me. I tried to move but I couldn't and the hounds knocked me over. I could see their open jaws and tearing teeth, but Bodo ran from the bushes and chased them away. Then he was gone, and I was alone with a wolf staring at me from the bushes. Searching desperately for my knife I couldn't find it. I tried to run but my boots were stuck to the path. The swirling tide crept towards me and lifted me off my feet.

The wolf was swimming towards me, its huge eyes glowing in the dark. My father was in a coracle and shouting. I caught hold of his hand, but the power of the sea tore me from him. Sinking beneath the waves into choking blackness, I woke with a terrible cry and didn't know where I was.

I lay there trembling and slowly recovering from my nightmare and noticed the fire was low. I found my clothes were almost dry, and I put them on, thinking I must have been asleep for some time. The sea salt had stained the fine cloak mother had embroidered for me, but it had a nice fresh smell and was now free from the filth of the rubbish pit.

Pulling it over my head because of the bent brooch clasp, I thought about the girl who had saved me from drowning and wondered if she had returned. I dragged on my boots without undoing the strings, and deciding to look for her, I was alarmed to hear someone in the narrow passageway.

A man was crouched low and coming towards me along the tunnel. He was dressed in black, and for one horrible moment, I thought it was Uhtred, but when he stepped down into the room and straightened his back, I saw a red-brown beard and hair that was thick and curly. He was so tall his head was close to the top of the beehive hut, his feet were bare, and he wore the cloak and robe of a Lindisfarne monk.

Glancing at me with piercing black eyes, his hooked nose reminded me of an owl's beak. In his arms was a willow basket full of small fish with silvery bodies, wet from the sea and marked with lemon spots. He nodded to me as if it were a natural thing to find a stranger in his home, placed the basket of fish on the floor, and sitting on a stool before the fire, I saw the shaven top of his head.

Silently inviting me to sit in the reeds at his feet, he must have noticed my swollen fingers, and taking a small pot from the top of the chest, he smeared green stuff on my cuts. I sniffed at it, there was a strong smell of seaweed, and wonderfully it took the stinging away.

Then he gutted the fish with a small sharp knife, threw the innards onto the fire, and piercing the fish with a stick, he placed them on stones in the hot ashes. It was a long time since I'd eaten Eacnung's stew and the smell of the sizzling fish made me very hungry, and when they were crisply brown, he put them on two wooden platters and handed one to me.

I broke my fish open and saw their firm white flesh. They smelled so good and tasted wonderful, and I gobbled my share down, breathing through my mouth to cool the hot flakes. The monk gave me dark bread from a flat loaf, full of half ground seeds, and handed me a beaker of golden liquid so sweet it made me cough and coated my tongue and teeth, but not unpleasantly.

'What is it?' I asked, wondering if the man would speak.

'Mead. The monks on Lindisfarne make it from honey,' he said, his voice surprising gentle.

The food and drink made my insides glow, and I wondered what to say to the stranger who had not scolded me when finding me uninvited in his home. I glanced around and my gaze fell on the cross by the wall.

'We have a cross at our meeting place,' I said. 'Like the one you have on your table. It has carvings of animals and birds on it, and my mother says it's there because of Saint Cuthbert, the good monk who lived in Northumbria more than a hundred years ago.'

'The table you see is called an altar, and my cross is driftwood,' the monk said, 'but it serves the same purpose.'

When the meal finished, we sat together in silence, and I listened to the cries of the gulls, the thunder of the sea against the cliffs, and was warm and comfortably full of food. The monk placed driftwood on the fire and I tried to watch him without staring too much, and as I cleaned the platters in a bucket of sand I said, 'Thank you for the food. I'm sorry I came into your home without asking.'

'You must save your thanks for Kendra,' he said. 'She pulled you from the sea and brought you here.'

'Kendra? I should very much like to thank her.'

He leaned forward to pick up more driftwood, and I noticed a golden chain and a large cross set with blood-red garnets, like the smaller ones I'd seen in my father's brooch. It was half-hidden in the folds of his cloak, and the stones glowed with a deep fire and I wondered how a monk living in a beehive hut came to have such a thing.

'Do you live here by yourself?' I dared to ask.

'You would think so, yes.'

'Aren't you lonely?'

'I chose to live like this.'

'Are you a hermit, or did you lose your family?'

He laughed and it was a warm and friendly sound. 'No, it's not sadness brings me here. I stay alone to pray and be close to God, ready to do his bidding.'

I was eager to ask him more questions, but he said, 'How did you come to be pulled from the sea?'

I told him about my family, how my father was on his way to Bamburgh to talk to the king, and about Uhtred. To speak about Bodo dying was hard. Then I told him how the Christian women were caring for my mother, grandmother, and my brother, and how I'd hoped to find shelter at the monastery on Lindisfarne.

When I paused for breath, he said, 'You were right to think of asking the monks to help you. They have no love for the Eorl, and they will let you know when it's safe to return to your settlement. I will take you to Lindisfarne, but be careful. Uhtred will kill you if he can.' Then he beckoned me from the hut and I followed him along the path to the cliff edge and was amazed to see he walked with a limp.

At last I'd found someone who struggled through life like me, and I felt warmth for the hermit who walked slowly and didn't make me feel useless. At the bottom of the steps, he led me across the beach and brought me to the entrance of a cave I hadn't noticed before. Half hidden by the cliffs, the sea had hollowed it out, and I followed him inside and saw a boat even larger than the one I'd been in with Kendra.

'Is it a coracle?' I asked, but he shook his head, and helping him push the heavy craft down the shingle, I saw it had an ox hide outer covering, two benches and oars, and a stout gunwale.

'It's a currach,' he said proudly, 'rowed many years ago by the monks from Ireland.' Pushing it into the sea, he hitched up his cloak and robe, struggled to lift one leg over the side of the boat, and helped me in after him. Then he sat on a bench, telling me to sit on the other behind him, and picking up one pair of oars, showed me how to slot mine through holes cut below the gunwale.

I'd never rowed before, but I anxiously watched what he did. Keeping the oars above the surface of the water, he leaned forward and lowered them into the sea. Then leaning back, he pulled the blades through the water and we moved forward. It wasn't easy at first, and I pulled gingerly with my injured hand, but to my surprise, there was little pain. My arms are strong and I learn most things quickly, and soon I was rowing with a good rhythm across the bay and we were heading for the narrow channel between the cliffs.

I looked nervously at the water pouring from the gap and swirling around us, and then I felt the currach picked up by the sucking tide and carried rapidly forward. I clung to the oars, scared the sea would tear them from my hands, but he steered the craft through the clouds of spray and water dashing against the cliff walls, and brought us safe from the channel into the open sea.

It looked such a long distance to Lindisfarne across the deep troughs and peaks of the restless waves. I shuddered, trying not to think about the deep, suffocating blackness beneath me, and made myself very busy with the rowing. Seals close to the cliffs joined us, some swimming ahead of the currach, others following behind. From time to time, their heads bobbed up close to the gunwale, and watching the monk with shining eyes, called to him eagerly in their harsh barking voices as we made steady progress towards the larger island.

The currach rode the waves well, the hermit guiding the fine craft towards the leeward side, and once in shallower water, I could see the land sloping down to a small beach. There were coracles tied to stakes well above the reach of the tide, and as we neared the shore, he shouted a warning.

The boat grated on the shingle and this time I was ready, and lowering myself safely over the side, I waded towards the beach. I turned to shout my thanks, but the noise of the crashing breakers carried my words away. He was rowing out into deeper water with the seals following the craft and he didn't seem to hear.

I waited until the currach was far into the distance, and then I looked up the slope from the beach and saw a well-used track through sandy soil. Grasping hold of marram grass, I began to climb the bank, and nearing the top, I was startled to see a pair of large muddy feet above me.

EIGHT

Kendra the Slave Girl

It was the girl from the sea. I scrambled up beside her and was glad to find I stood a head taller, though she seemed a bit older than me.

She'd slotted a knife through a strip of animal hide round her rough tunic, and she looked very strong. She had the appearance of our slaves at home, but I was puzzled because of her long plait. Slaves have cropped hair and I wondered if she was a runaway from a nearby settlement and her hair had grown.

She was staring at me, her green eyes widening, and there was a gap between her large front teeth. 'Sea washed you up?' she said.

She reached out to touch my cloak, woven by mother from the softest wool. I thought she was making fun of me and I didn't like it, but how could I be angry with someone who had pulled me from the sea?

'You'd best come along with me,' the girl said. 'Abbot Higbald sees to pilgrims, even those who nearly drown getting here. You're a funny sort of pilgrim, never seen the likes of you before.' She poked me in the belly with a rough finger, and she smelled strongly of onions. 'What's your name, eh? I'm Kendra.'

'Toland. I'm not a pilgrim,' I said stiffly, hoping I sounded important like father. I wasn't sure what a pilgrim was, but I didn't want her to know she knew more than me. 'I must speak to the abbot, you must take me there!'

'Haven't killed anyone now, have you?' Kendra said, staring at me as though she wanted to see inside my head. 'Don't owe no blood debt for those you have slain, do you? Not that your look is anything to go by.' She sniffed, rubbing her short nose on the sleeve of her tunic. 'You might be a real villain in disguise.' Then she laughed, hard and long. 'Well, maybe not in that finery.'

The girl's voice rose and fell in a singing way, and many of our slaves had the same singing voice. My father told me they came from the Welsh mountain wars and gave themselves into slavery rather than starve with their homes destroyed and the long winter approaching.

She ran off along the stony track through rough pasture, and I couldn't keep up with her and looking back at me curiously, she saw me limping. 'What's wrong with you?' she asked abruptly. Then frowning she turned away, gave a low whistle, and shouted, 'Here, boy,' and something bounded through the dried willow herb towards her.

It was a lurcher with long spindle legs, his soft grey coat covered with grass seeds, and my heart thudded in my chest and I stretched out my hands to him, but he took no notice. Stupidly I'd hoped it was my hound Bodo, and I felt sad as she patted the dog prancing around her.

'You like my Modig, then?' she said, fondling the animal's soft domed head and singing words to it in the same strange language our slaves used to each other.

'I thought for a moment – never mind,' I said, tears stinging under my eyelids. I longed to touch the hound and was overjoyed when he gently licked the back of my hand and let me stroke his head.

'There's lots of hares round here,' she said. 'He's swift when need be.'

I nodded, scrubbing at my eyes with my knuckles when she wasn't watching. I was thinking about days with father and Bodo, coursing the wild hares, but she was already striding off and speaking to her dog and he scampered away. I followed her, wading through thistles and wild oats, and we came to a field where a monk, with his robe hitched up to his knees, was driving an ox harnessed to an ard and cutting the soft sandy soil.

'That's one of them from the monastery,' Kendra said. 'They're out working in the fields when they're not doing their singing.' She sniffed. 'Not real singing.'

Beyond the field, and enclosed within a long fence, were the monastery's wooden buildings with thatched roofs like those of my settlement. One was finer than the rest, the only one built of stone, and it had a cross on one gable end and a small arch with a bell hanging from it at the other.

'That's the church,' she said, reluctantly stopping to let me catch up and pointing to the stone cross on the roof. 'You'll not speak to the monks now, not the proper ones anyway, they're at their prayers. At it all day, several times a day, they are. Have to drop tools when they're working in the fields and hear the bell, less they have permission not too. Funny to see them lift their robes and run like old women,' she said, hooting with laughter. 'In the night too, they're always ringing that bell for prayers. Nuisance thing wakes me but you get used to it. The monks mean well, treat us slaves kindly enough.'

She pointed to a group of beehive huts beyond the fence, like the one on Inner Farne, but built of wood and thatch. 'There's where they sleep,' she said, 'and that's where they eat together,' and I saw a cluster of larger wooden buildings on the other side of the enclosure.

'There's the kitchen, next to where the monks take care of their sick – they don't just care for their own kind, they heal the slaves too – I've seen them do it,' she said, as if daring me to say I didn't believe her.

Looking across the island towards the place where the sun sinks each night into the sea, I saw huts built of turf, and close by were men, women, and children, digging and weeding in the fields.

'Those over there, they're slaves like me. The monks gave us our freedom,' said Kendra. 'Still, we stay to work – it's better than wandering the roads with nothing to eat, and the monks are good to us. One day, though, I think we'll leave, go back to our own land. Nothing like your own land, however good people are to you,' she said thoughtfully.

'What's that?' I said quickly, not wanting to think about Uhtred attacking our settlement and taking all we had. I pointed to one house next to the kitchen, bigger than the rest.

'The long house? It's where the monks spend most of their day copying their holy books, when it's not their turn in the fields.'

'I'd like to see the books,' I said. 'My mother told me a story she'd heard from her great-grandmother about a holy book Saint Cuthbert always carried with him.'

'Never heard of it,' she said cheerfully, and led me through a gate into the enclosure. Then seeing a goose feather she picked it up, pulling the silky barbs between her fingers. 'The monks use feathers for writing their books – one day they might teach me to read.'

She led the way to the church and I was amazed to see how well the stones fitted together, and up close saw the small high window places filled with pieces of coloured glass, like the beads in my mother's jewellery box.

'The monks pray to their God – never stop,' she said with a puzzled frown. 'Now they're doing their singing.'

I listened for the sound of a harp, but all I heard were men's voices, rising and falling, and it was not like music I'd ever known.

'They do that singing a lot – funny sort of noise, a bit like talking, but expect they need to do it. They don't speak much – hardly say a word to each other.' She sniffed again. 'Spend most of their time saying nowt.' She listened for a while. 'There, they've stopped, so they'll soon be finished. Best be taking you to Abbot Higbald when it's over – but sometimes the old monks do go on a bit.'

As she spoke, the heavy oak door of the church opened slowly, and the monks crossed the enclosure, walking one behind the other with their hoods over their faces and their hands pushed deep in the sleeves

71

of their black robes. We followed them to the long house where the shutters stood back from the window places, and when the monks were gone inside, I went with Kendra to the door.

She pushed me forward, hissing at me to knock, but before I could do it, the door jerked open and a head, bald with a grey frill of stiff hair like broom twigs, popped out. I jumped back nervously, and the monk stared at my sea-stained cloak and silently beckoned with his hand. I turned to Kendra to see if she would come with me, and to my surprise, she'd gone.

Stepping through the door into shafts of sunlight streaming from the window places was like entering one of my happy dreams. The ones where I can walk like other people and can run and jump. In the soft light were rows of tall, narrow tables, and sitting at each was a monk perched on a high stool. The sloping tabletops had a strange collection of thin pieces of dried animal skin, goose feathers, clay bottles, and pestles and mortars, some filled with black ashes. In other bowls were pastes of scarlet, deep glowing blue, and yellow like the golden heart of the kingcup, and I wanted to stop and stare.

I had to be careful where I trod, for on the floor were small barrels with skins floating in a strange milky liquid. Stretched on frames against the wall were more skins, and despite the pungent smell stinging my nostrils, it was a peaceful place. Motes of dust danced in the sunlight and the monks' sandaled feet shuffled on the scrubbed wooden floor. Tiny pieces of gold and silver, beaten thin, wafted gently from the tables as I passed, and the monks made anxious darting movements to catch them and angrily glared at me. I hurried away and the monk with hair like twigs led me from one room to another, and reaching a door near the end of the building he opened it, told me Abbot Higbald was within, and gave me a push.

The room was small and cramped, with shelves full of dyed animal skins wrapped round bundles of something I couldn't see and I wondered if they were the books Kendra told me about. Thinking the monk who'd brought me there was wrong, and I was alone, I jumped nervously when I noticed a small man watching me. I could just see his head above a table piled with more bundles, and I looked down nervously at his shaven crown. He rose from his stool, but he didn't seem to get much bigger and his large silver cross hung below his belt.

The abbot had a weathered face with no beard and the bright round eyes of a bird. He stared at me from head to foot, studying my mother's fine stitching on my stained cloak, my boots made especially for me with one sole thicker than the other one, and the silver decoration on my brooch.

'I see you are interested in our books,' he said, and with small neat hands removed one from a shelf and held it out to me. He told me the monks made the covers from calfskin, and this one had a pale cream cover decorated with thin strips of gold, the colour of my mother's ring.

'It's wonderful,' I said, not daring to touch it.

Returning it to the shelf, he abruptly asked me what brought me to

Lindisfarne, and not knowing where to begin, I blurted out that I wished to stay on the island until I had news of my father. Then I told him about Uhtred threatening to kill my people and how I'd escaped with my family through the forest and how they were now safe with the nuns at Ancroft.

The abbot was silent for a while, and then he gave a long sigh. 'Yes, the Eorl Uhtred is an evil man. He comes often to Lindisfarne, searching for the necklace that once belonged to his mother Juliana, who died last year. He says his mother promised to give him the necklace as a keepsake, and his father had no right to steal it to pay a blood debt.'

'Where is the necklace now?' I asked, remembering my uncle Siward's words that Uhtred would not stop his killing until he found the thing he searched for.

The abbot gave me a secretive look. 'The Eorl would ransack the church to find it, but he does not dare whilst King Aethelred protects us. However, with the king gone from Bamburgh, I fear it will not be long before the Eorl's huscarls break down the door of our church and desecrate the holy place.'

I shuddered. 'Is the king away still?' I asked nervously. 'My father needs urgently to speak with him.'

'One of the monks returned with news from the border and says the king fights the Mercian armies. That was a month ago. Two monks are on their way back from the church in Durham, and hopefully, they will bring news of the king and you may learn what has happened to

74

your father. However, something puzzles me. How did you reach us? It is high tide, and by your cloak I should think you were caught by the sea.'

'Early this morning, Uhtred's men were chasing me and I was swept out to sea. I would have drowned, but Kendra your slave girl pulled me into her coracle and saved my life. She took me to Inner Farne, and the monk living there brought me here.'

The abbot looked at me keenly, his eyes searching my face. 'Tell me about this monk. There has not been anyone living in the hermit's shelter on the island for many years. What sort of man is he?'

'He is tall with a high forehead and a mass of thick reddish brown hair and he has a beard.' I thought for a moment. 'He wears a cross with garnets.'

The abbot eagerly beckoned me to follow him from the long house, and I hurried as fast as my leg would allow as he ran across the enclosure to the church. By the time I reached the door and looked inside, coloured fragments of light from the window places were dancing around him and I heard the soft swish of his cloak brushing the stone floor.

The abbot's sandaled feet slapped on the empty paving as he moved swiftly down the church, and catching up with him he pointed to a painting on the wall behind the altar, the surface dark with age. I could just make out the shadowy form of a monk with a long beard, and round his neck was a cross with four curving arms set with garnets.

'Yes, that looks like the hermit on Inner Farne,' I said. 'He lives in a hut on top of the cliffs, and he rows a boat he calls a currach, not a coracle.'

The abbot sighed and shook his head. 'I'm a foolish old man to dream such dreams. You are mistaken. This painting is of Saint Cuthbert and he died many years ago. The monk you saw may be Benedictine, but he must be from another religious house, further down the coast, and taken to living in Cuthbert's old hermitage.'

His quiet voice mumbled on, and I noticed a book on the white linen cloth covering the altar and it was the most perfect thing I'd ever seen. It had a pale rose coloured calfskin cover with a twisted clasp of gold and silver. Decorating the cover was a cross of the same metals, and between the arms of the cross, precious gemstones glinted in the light spilling from the window places.

'I see you are admiring the holy book of Lindisfarne. Abbot Eadfrith made this copy in memory of our good Saint Cuthbert. Inside are the four stories that tell of our Lord's time here on earth. We call them the four gospels.'

'Those shining stones!' I said.

The abbot smiled in his secretive way. 'They are from Juliana's necklace.'

He gently undid the book's delicate clasp, and inside the cover were thinnest animal skins. They were covered with swirling shapes and brightly painted animals and birds, their scarlet, gold, and emerald bodies very like the creatures on our stone cross at home.

I stepped near to look at them better and knocked my leg against something hard. On the stone floor beside the altar was a coffin of roughly hewn wood, and it had carvings of people with wings, but I didn't like the look of it.

'Saint Cuthbert's bones,' the abbot said.

'Why is it here?' I asked. 'Surely, he should be buried?'

'He is here, resting on Lindisfarne where he spent most of his life – where he belongs to be.'

'But–'

'You think he is what you call *dead* and we should be rid of him? The saint is still with us and works many miracles of healing. We see no difference between life and death. It is all one to us. Those whom people think of as dead are still with us, although we cannot see them.'

He gave one last glance at the painting of Saint Cuthbert, and shook his head. Then walking towards the door, I followed him, and stepping from the softly coloured church shadows into sunlight, I looked across the fields and thought I saw a coracle bobbing on the sea.

'Please,' I said, 'do you know where Kendra is?'

'Kendra?'

'Yes, the slave girl who saved me from drowning.'

'I have never heard that name. If she is a slave, you'll probably find her with her people at work in the fields.'

I thanked the abbot, and in the pale sunlight with gulls circling

77

above me I felt better, for he'd given me permission to stay on the island and had promised to tell me if the monks brought news of my father. Limping across the fields to search for Kendra, it wasn't long before I saw her and Modig coming towards me on the path, and she was carrying a reed basket over her arm.

Proudly showing me dry bread with squashed blackberries sticking to it, and a jug of sour goat's milk, she said, 'You can have some if you like,' and I thought of the bright fish the hermit had cooked and stared at what she offered in disgust.

'That's all there is,' she said angrily, 'if you don't want it, I'll eat it myself.' She had such a threatening angry face that I hastily thanked her, and sitting beside her on the grass her lurcher came and snuffed at me. His whiskers tickled and made me laugh, and I threw most of my bread to him when she wasn't watching, and he gulped it down as eagerly as Bodo would have done.

'My dog Bodo was a greedy eater,' I said, trying to chew what was left of the tough bread. I drank some of the sour milk from the jug, shuddered, and asked if there were any more blackberries.

'There's lots on the banks of the Lough. It's fresh water – close to the cliffs. If you want blackberries there's plenty there, but you'll have to pick them yourself.'

She scrambled to her feet and this time she walked more slowly down the sandy track, though not much, and Modig followed at her heels. We passed a row of beehives and heard the bees beating their wings to keep warm, and there was a dip in the land and steep banks with a mere in the hollow and the sea beyond.

Modig ran through the reeds to the water's edge and clouds of black-headed gulls rose in the air, darkening the sky and filling the air with their deafening clamour. Kendra called to him but he took no notice, and we followed the path round the mere where bramble sprays were laden with ripe blackberries. Eagerly stuffing fruit into my mouth, and hoping to take away the taste of the rancid goat's milk, I heard a dull thud that seemed to shake the ground and Modig barked.

'It came from the beach,' Kendra said, turning to me in alarm. 'Let's go look.'

'No,' I said, pulling her back, 'it might be dangerous,' but she shook me off and walked up the slope from the mere, and reluctantly I followed her. Reaching the top of the bank, she dropped to the ground, moving forward on her belly. I did the same and wriggled after her to the cliff edge, and peering over, I came face to face with the head of an enormous dragon!

Its long neck stretched towards me and it glared at me with wild red eyes, smoke drifted from its mouth, and it flapped its blood stained wings.

NINE

A Dragon on the Beach

Terrified, I struggled to my feet. Kendra raced down the track and across the fields towards the monastery, with Modig barking at her heels.

Looking fearfully behind me, and hoping it would take the dragon a long time to climb the path to the top of the cliff, I forgot that dragons could fly. Frantic to escape from it, I was fighting for breath when I reached the gate into the enclosure and panted, 'Dragon – a dragon – a dragon on the beach!'

The monks were gathering around Kendra, and one man, older than the rest, caught me by the shoulder. 'Now, now, slowly,' he said sternly, looking from Kendra to me. 'You make no sense, shouting like this.'

'It's a *dragon* – a dragon on the beach,' Kendra exclaimed. 'On the other side of the mere – we saw it!'

'A fearsome – it was fearsome,' I gasped. My lungs ached with the violence of hurling myself over the fields, and I lifted up my hands to show how big the creature was.

'Yes, yes,' the monk said, and he smiled and winked at a young man with his head unshaven and wearing a short robe over leggings. 'Desmond, go with these young people and discover what they have seen.'

The monk called Desmond smiled broadly and brushed his floppy hair from his face. 'Take me to where you saw the dragon,' he said. 'Though I think it's too pleasant an afternoon for any monster to come visiting.'

'It's true,' I said angrily. 'We saw it – we saw its terrible head, its wings covered in blood and smoke coming from its mouth!'

'You must show me,' the monk said, and noticing my leg, began to walk slowly along the path with Kendra telling him to take care, and me limping after them with Modig trotting by my side. Stories of scaly dragons rising from the waves, and pulling unwary seafarers to their lairs at the bottom of the sea, came into my head, and when we reached the mere, I hung back. I didn't want the dragon to grab me and tear me to pieces, and I tugged at Desmond's robe and urged him to take care.

The monk grinned at me, and saying he would come to no harm, dropped to his knees and crawled forward and Kendra called after him that it was too dangerous. I waited with Modig, hardly daring to watch as Desmond moved slowly towards the edge of the cliff, and I held my breath, expecting the dragon to eat him as he cautiously peered over.

Then I heard him whistle softly. 'Come and see,' he said, turning his head to nod at us. 'There is your threatening dragon. What you saw is a long boat – though one far bigger than any I have seen before.'

Still fearful, we crawled to the cliff edge and peering down saw a boat's high prow, carved into the shape of a magnificent dragon's head. The painted eyes were bold and threatening, and the red and white striped sail flapped and cracked in the strong wind. Along the gunwale were many wooden shields with the leather covers bright with paint, and the metal bosses glinting. Smoke curled up from a driftwood fire and I saw men as tall and powerful as my father, wearing helmets and chain mail shirts. They were heaving on stout ropes and dragging the wide bottomed craft up the beach, all the while calling to each other in a strange tongue I'd never heard before.

'We must welcome them as we do all visitors to these shores,' Desmond said, his eyes shining with excitement. 'Kendra, run and let the abbot know so a feast may be prepared. These men must have travelled far across the sea.'

'No,' I said, pulling at his arm, 'they are armed like warriors, ready for battle. See the swords they carry. They might do you harm!'

Kendra shouted at the monk in her own language, holding him back, but he shook her off, jumped to his feet, and disappeared down the steep path to the beach. We watched nervously until we saw him again at the bottom of the cliff, striding out across the sand, and one of the warriors shouted and hurried towards him. The monk opened his arms in greeting and the warrior drew his sword, running him through. The young man toppled forward on his knees with blood soaking through his robe and fell face down into the sand.

Kendra made an angry growling noise in her throat. Then calling to her dog she dragged me back towards the mere and as we stumbled along she panted, 'I've heard about them…the hermit warned me…these must be the men coming from the north to steal and murder…..'

Her words filled me with horror, and we were not far from the enclosure when we heard terrifying yells behind us. Turning round, I saw men from the dragon boat chasing the slaves across the fields, and Kendra shrieked, 'The Northmen are coming! The Northmen are coming! They have killed Desmond!'

The monks working in the fields ran towards the sea and others came from the long house into the enclosure, some helping those who were old or ill. I heard Abbot Higbald shouting they must save Saint Cuthbert's gospels. He ran to the church and we followed the monks with Modig racing ahead, and stumbling through the door, one man locked and bolted it behind us.

The abbot seized a heavy silver cross from the altar, and holding it before him ran to the door crying, 'Deliver us O Lord, from the fury of the Northmen, deliver us O Lord, from the fury of the Northmen!'

I heard shouts and running footsteps coming towards the church. Axe heads thudded against the stout oak of the door making me shake with fright and there were terrifying screams. I smelled burning thatch, heard a loud crackling and a frightening whoosh above my head, and thick smoke drifted under the door and swirled round my feet.

'Quick,' a monk shouted at me, the one who sent poor Desmond to his death, 'follow me.' Hurrying to the back wall of the church, as fast as his old body would allow, he picked up a tall candlestick. Fear giving him strength, he swung it and smashed the coloured glass in the small window above the painting of St. Cuthbert.

Then snatching up the book covered with Juliana's jewels from the altar, he thrust it into my hands. 'This book is more precious than your life – you must bring it safely to the monks at the White Church – close by the monastery at Durham!'

Modig was barking, screams from the enclosure froze my blood, and I heard the church door splintering. The old monk looked wildly towards the door and said fiercely, 'Swear you'll do this! Swear on the holy book that you will guard it with you life!' He seized my wrist and slammed my hand hard onto the surface of the gospels, the jewels digging into my flesh, and I shouted, 'I swear! I swear!'

Fragments of burning thatch were floating around him, and the monk cried, 'Go quick – squeeze through the window space – drop down into the bushes. We shall pray the smoke will hide you!'

Stuffing the book inside my tunic, I tightened my belt to keep it safe. Climbing onto the altar, I pulled Kendra after me, and seeing a silver and bronze cup I used it to shatter the shards of glass sticking up around the window. Reaching for the stone ledge, I lifted myself over it and fell to the ground. Bruised and winded, I saw Modig leap through the opening with Kendra struggling behind him, and pushing frantically to force her shoulders through the narrow gap, she landed heavily beside me.

'We must get to the coracles,' she said urgently, and we crept warily through the smoke, trying to keep together and fearful the Northmen would catch us. We were tripping over Modig, and we'd only gone a few paces when we could no longer see the wall of the church and it was impossible to know where we were.

'I think it's this way!' Kendra insisted, but I was sure she was wrong. We were frantically arguing, trying to pull each other in different directions, when we bumped into the enclosure fence and scrambled over it into the fields.

Flames were shooting through the roof of the long house, the church roof was on fire, and terrified, I clutched at my tunic to make sure the holy book was still there. Limping as fast as I could after Kendra and Modig through the blinding smoke, I followed them along the track with the terrible shouts and cries from the enclosure ringing in my head. Scared the others would leave me behind, I stumbled painfully forward, trying to keep on my feet, and gasped with relief when I heard the sound of waves breaking and crashing on the shore.

Through a gap in the billowing clouds of smoke I saw the beach where the hermit had brought me earlier in the day and Kendra cried, 'I'll see if it's safe!' and disappeared down the slope with her dog sliding after her.

I waited nervously, but it wasn't long before I heard her climbing back up the bank and she growled, 'The coracles have gone, the monks have taken them! We'll follow the path round the coast to the crossing place – we can't stay here – we'd best keep moving!'

Surrounded by a drifting wall of smoke I listened fearfully to the distant shouts of the Northmen and tried to keep up with her. Unable to see one another, Kendra was calling to me and I followed the sound of her voice, tripping on rough ground and struggling across the fields, but it was hopeless, we didn't know where we were going.

Afraid of plunging over the edge of a cliff, I heard angry shouts that seemed to be coming closer. Thinking the Northmen had discovered us, I stumbled in one direction and then another and saw someone on the track in front of me. Terrified, I was feeling for my knife when a strong wind lifted the smoke, carrying it away from the island, and I was startled and relieved to see it was Kendra.

'We've taken the wrong path!' she cried in alarm.

Looking hurriedly around, I saw she was right. We were on the cliff top, not far from the mere where I'd picked the blackberries, and a group of Northmen were yelling at slaves, pigs, and goats, and driving them towards the steep path to the beach.

'Get down!' Kendra warned, but too late, a bearded warrior let out a fierce bellow and raced across the cliff top, a double-headed axe clenched in his fist.

Kendra dragged me after her and I shouted at her to run and save herself. The Northman grabbed my arm and Kendra clung on to me and wouldn't let go. He swung his fist and punched her in the belly, she doubled up and fell, and I kicked him and tried to escape. With a roar of anger, he grabbed me by my belt. Swinging me round, the precious book fell from my tunic and slid over the edge of the cliff.

I cried out in despair and Modig raced along the track and fastened his sharp teeth in the warrior's leg. The man howled and swung his axe at the dog and I yelled in fear. Modig jumped away and the axe embedded itself in the ground. Returning swiftly to the attack, the dog leapt into the air, fastened his teeth in the Northman's wrist, and dangled from his arm.

Kendra staggered to her feet and hurled a fistful of sand and pebbles in the Northman's face. Letting go of me, the warrior clawed at his eyes, screaming in pain. The dog loosed his grip, there was the flash of a blade, and Kendra struck the warrior between his helmet and his chain mail shirt. He tottered back, his huge body crashed amongst the thistles, and he lay horribly still.

'I don't think he'll worry us again,' she said, wiping her knife on the grass, sticking it back in her belt, and patting her dog's head.

Shocked by what had happened, I stared at the slain warrior, unable to move, and Kendra shook me. 'Come on,' she said urgently, 'the Northmen went down to the beach, but we'd better be quick – there may be more of them!' and she started to drag me along the track but I pushed her away.

'The monks' holy book – it fell over the cliff! I must go back – I have to find it!'

'No one will know it was *you* lost it. The monks won't blame you, if there are any left to tell that is. Anyway, it weren't your fault!'

I took no notice and limped away and she shouted, 'Don't be daft! How do you think you'll find it without the Northmen seeing you? Do you want to end up a slave like me? They'll take you with them and make you work, and it's no use, the tide's coming in and the book's probably in the sea!'

She ran after me, and I was struggling to free myself from her clutching hands when she shouted, 'Look!' and pointed out to sea. Already some distance from the shore, I saw the flash of many oars as the warriors rowed the dragon's head boat into deeper water, and the wind was beginning to tug at the red and white sail.

'Well, they've going and they don't look as if they're coming back,' she said, 'and I suppose you won't change your daft mind till you've searched for the monks' book.' Giving me a shake, she called to Modig, and still muttering about the waste of time, she returned along the track and reluctantly helped me down the path to the beach.

I waded awkwardly through the soft sand, anxious to begin the search and worrying about the tide with Modig trotting happily through the ripples on the shore. At first, I didn't think it would take long to find the gospels, but there were so many large boulders scattered at the bottom of the cliffs and it was hard to clamber over them. Dragging myself along and slipping into rock pools, I was tired and bad tempered and beginning to give up hope.

Kendra had stopped looking for the book and was throwing bits of seaweed for Modig to catch, and I was annoyed with her for not helping me when I saw a heap of charred wood on the sand. 'There's the Northmen's fire,' I shouted, 'and the gully where the dragon boat rested. We *must* be somewhere near the place where the warrior caught me and the book fell over the cliff.'

Thinking about the Northman and his double-edged axe, I suddenly remembered Desmond and looked fearfully around for his body. 'Where's the monk?' I said. 'What do you think happened to Desmond?'

'Maybe the tide carried him out to sea, he was over there when the Northman struck him – the water's already covered that bit.'

Trying to forget what happened to the young monk, and with the tide creeping up the beach, I called angrily to Kendra to come and search.

'If I don't, I suppose we'll be here all night,' she grumbled. Then unwillingly she joined me, and we hunted until the cliffs cast long shadows and our eyes ached from staring at the sand.

By now, the tide had covered most of the beach and I said miserably, 'It's no good, we'll never find it, it's probably been washed out to sea with Desmond. I swore on the holy book to take it to the White Church and now I've lost it. What am I going to do?'

TEN

A Promise Not Kept

I sat down on a boulder, the pain in my leg gnawing at me like a dog with a bone and watching the tide rapidly retreating. 'I've lost the gospels and I've failed the monks,' I said bitterly. 'They gave their lives to save Cuthbert's book and now it's for nothing.'

'Don't be daft,' said Kendra. 'You didn't harm the book, see. The Northman did. It was Cuthbert's book and I'm sure he wouldn't blame you, not after he went telling everyone to be loving and forgiving.'

'How do you know? How do you know he wouldn't blame me?' I said angrily.

'I know lots more than you,' she said. 'We slaves listen, hear things.'

She sat on the sand with Modig beside her and began skimming stones across the tops of the waves. 'That's a good one,' she said, watching it bounce. Then she was quiet and after a while she said, 'I hope some of the slaves escaped back to the mountains.'

'I'm sure they did,' I said quickly, wondering if she was thinking about her family. I'd been so busy worrying about my own people I had selfishly forgotten to ask about hers.

'Your parents – are they...' I hesitated, but she didn't speak, and I thought how brave she was if she didn't have a family. At least my family were safe with the nuns and one day I'd be with them again and father would return. Sitting beside Kendra, and wondering what my kinsfolk were doing, and looking out to sea, I noticed a small boat coming towards the beach and Modig jumped up and barked.

'There,' I said, struggling to stand up. 'Can you see? Who do you think it is?'

'Well it's not the dragon boat if that's what you're worrying about. Seems like a coracle or a currach to me – oh, it's the hermit – the hermit from Inner Farne.'

When the currach was close to the shore I saw many seals swimming beside it, and I watched nervously as the black robed monk stumbled onto the sand. Kendra rushed to help him drag the craft from the water, but I hung back, scared to let him know about my promise and that I'd lost the gospels.

The seals followed him, bouncing up the beach on their flippers like eager dogs. Barking in their deep voices and licking his feet, he stopped to speak to them, and with annoyed grunts the creatures reluctantly shuffled back to the sea. Feeling anxious, I watched him crossing the sand towards me and gave a cry of fear and joy, for in his hand he carried the holy book of Lindisfarne.

'I found this floating not far from the shore,' he said with a heavy frown, his eyes dark above the beaked nose looking suddenly fierce.

'It was the Northman – he attacked us,' Kendra said, quick to defend me. 'Toland was taking the book to Durham and it fell off the cliff when the Northman caught him – it wasn't his fault.'

91

'The book – the book fell from my tunic,' I stammered, hardly daring to look at the hermit. 'I promised the monks I'd take it to the White Church – we've been searching and searching!'

He held out the gospels and I was amazed to see only the edges of the delicate animal skins damaged by seawater.

'Keep your promise to the monks,' was all he said, although he still looked angry, and gratefully I slipped Cuthbert's book inside my tunic and once more tightened my belt.

'Do you know if the monks – did they escape from the church?' I dared to ask, although sadly I thought I knew the answer.

The hermit shook his head. 'Not from the church, but some reached the coracles, taking as many books as they could carry. They returned later to find Saint Cuthbert's coffin had miraculously survived. If you keep your vow to carry the gospels to the White Church, then those who have died will not have done so in vain.'

He looked at me solemnly, and I found his gaze hard to return. 'Many books were destroyed in the fire, and it takes the monks a long weary time to copy them,' he said. 'Each one is precious, but the one you carry is written with more love and care, and more beautifully decorated than the rest, and therefore is the most treasured.'

I nodded and this time he spoke more gently. 'The tide is over the crossing place. I'll take you around the coast to the mainland and you may continue your journey.'

'Please,' I said, worried about the awful task ahead of me, 'could you tell me how I shall find the White Church?'

'Follow the road south towards the fortress. If you ask at Bamburgh village you may find someone to guide you to Durham.'

I nodded, although I feared it would be hard to find anyone willing to help me at the village, and Kendra was already pushing the currach back into the sea. Settling on one of the benches, she took the oars, calling to me and ready to row into deeper water. I waded into the sea, scrambled over the gunwale after the hermit, and sat on the floor of the boat close to her feet. Then putting my arm around Modig, I felt him bristle, and he barked at the seals as they swam along side.

'I wish I knew how he does it,' I whispered to Kendra as we moved away from the beach and the seals swarmed around us. They were excitedly lifting their heads close to the currach and some were floating on their backs, holding gleaming fish between their flippers and using their smooth bellies like a table as they ate their catch.

'Does what?' Kendra asked with her back bent as she dipped the oars into the sea.

'Makes the seals follow him.'

'He doesn't make them. They love him and want to be with him,' she said, and I was thinking how strange these sea creatures. Yet Modig loved Kendra, and I loved Bodo still. I sighed and stroked Modig's head.

Kendra and the hermit rowed steadily, fighting their way through the turbulent crosscurrents around the island, and it wasn't long until I saw the mainland and the line of stakes marking the crossing place, now beneath the sea. Shuddering, and thankful I had no need to battle with the tide, I noticed the dunes and the Bamburgh road coming closer. I was worried about the rest of my journey, and how I would find Durham, and the currach was moving all too quickly towards the shore.

Unhappily lowering myself over the gunwale into the waves, I struggled through the shingle onto the beach, wondering miserably what would happen to me now I was on my own. A deep sadness gripped me when I realised I might never see Kendra and the hermit again, and stumbling onto dry sand, I turned to call goodbye and heard Kendra shout, 'Wait for me!'

She leapt from the boat and splashed through the sea towards me with Modig swimming after her and I could hardly believe my good fortune. The hound ran across the sand, shaking his coat, spraying me with salt water, and bouncing round me. Patting him, I struggled to find the words to tell her how pleased I was she was coming with me and I tried to give her a hug, but she roughly pushed me away.

Hurriedly shouting my thanks to the hermit, I saw he was already far from the shore and rowing towards the distant Farne islands and I hoped he had heard me. Then touching the holy book inside my tunic to make sure it was still there, I followed Kendra and Modig into the sand hills with a wonderful safe feeling inside me.

With her helping me through the soft sliding dunes, it didn't take long before we climbed out onto the Bamburgh road. There was no one about, and after we'd walked a long tiring way, I noticed Elwick village close to the shore and the track my mother, brother, and grandmother had taken with Siward to Ancroft. I desperately wanted to stop and ask my uncle about my family, but Kendra shook her head and called me to hurry, saying there were dark clouds coming and we must reach Bamburgh before nightfall.

It wasn't until Modig found a stream trickling across the heath, and we stopped for a drink, that I had a chance to sit down for a while. I was still longing to take the path to the village, and becoming more and more miserable. Watching Modig chasing after a grey plover, I was about to say I must go back and see my uncle, when Kendra pulled me to my feet, saying, 'Come on, it's getting late. Modig will find us when he's ready.'

Still thinking about Elwick, I limped wearily along the road, and we hadn't gone far when I looked across the heath to the forest and saw we were close to the track that led to my settlement.

'What's wrong?' she said, looking round, 'what are you waiting for?'

'Over there. There's a path to my settlement!'

'You promised to take the book to the White Church. You've no time for that,' she said crossly. 'It won't be long before dark.'

'We can do both – I just want to see if my kinsfolk are well and if my father has returned. It won't take long,' I pleaded. 'I have to see if my father is safe!'

She shook her head and kept walking. Telling myself it was only a short distance to the settlement and that I could still carry the holy book to Durham, I called to her again. She took no notice, and filled with an unbearable need to return home, I left the road and stumbled across the heath.

I could hear her shouting angrily but the further I went the more eager I was to find my father. Forgetting the gospels in my tunic and my promise to the monks, I hurried towards the forest. Kendra was shouting but I didn't stop. Then I heard her running behind me and when she caught up, she walked along in silence.

We were close to the forest, but thinking about wolves, I followed the track around the foot of the hill, walking through fields of winter barley stirring restlessly in the wind. This took much longer than I thought and I limped along as fast as I could. Kendra was muttering angrily, and I was anxiously looking for the settlement when she came to a halt in front of me and shouted, 'You shouldn't be doing this! You should keep your promise and take the book to the White Church. Go back!'

I knew she was right and that made me angry with myself as much as with her. 'We're not far now - we shall soon be at the palisade,' I said, and she growled at me and shook her fist, but she let me pass and didn't leave me.

With pain shooting up my leg, I limped along the track, and hurrying away from her and fearful she would try to stop me again, I saw the pigpens and the pig keeper's shelter and cried out in relief. By now, I was close enough to see the palisade, but I slowed to a halt and then stood still in horror, for all that was visible were charred timbers.

Many of the houses and workshops had been set on fire and my house was gone. Raw timber patches on the few houses remaining looked strange against the burned, blackened oak. The gatehouse had fallen and there was a roughly repaired bridge across the ditch.

Full of despair, and with Kendra close behind me, I crossed the bridge, and seeing a woman carrying a bundle of wood I called after her shouting, 'My father – is he here?'

I limped towards her and she stopped and looked at me open mouthed. Men, working to rebuild one of the houses came hurrying towards me, running through clouds of black ash, and the man who led them was Heolstor, my father's brother.

His face was twisted with anger, and he shouted, 'Be gone, you useless creature. I thought to be rid of you forever! I told Uhtred where to find you, thinking to save my people, but the villain didn't keep his word. When his dogs didn't sniff you out, he came back in the night, burned down our homes, and killed many of our kinsfolk!'

'Where is my Father?' I said, not flinching from his clenched fist.

'Can't you see?' he bellowed. 'Can't you see what your father has done? If he'd accepted Uhtred as hearth lord, we'd still have our homes. Those of us who managed to escape have lost everything, the beasts are gone, the crops destroyed–'

'Go, before we kill you.' It was the carpenter, full of cold rage, and men dropped their tools, crowding round me, and I feared for my life.

'It was not my father's fault,' I shouted at them.

'The coward Godwin dare not show his face again,' the carpenter growled, raising his axe, but I stood my ground. If they were going to slaughter me then I must be my father's son and show no fear, and I hid my trembling hands behind my back.

'Your Father ran off to save his own skin,' another man shouted.

'The coward left us to face Uhtred and his mercenaries to save himself, but it did him no good – he's dead!' It was Oswold, Heolstor's son, and he picked up a stone and flung it at me.

I ducked, protecting myself with my arms, and thinking it was the end of me another voice rang high and clear. It was Heolstor's wife, running towards me with Kendra by her side.

'Will killing Toland bring back those who have died, or our animals and crops?' the woman said angrily, pushing between the men around me. 'Hasn't there been enough killing? This boy has done you no harm.'

She took hold of me by my cloak, and before the men could stop her, dragged me across the yard towards the bridge. 'Go now, quick as you can,' she hissed in my ear. 'Or it won't be long before they kill you whatever I say. Go!'

I limped through the fallen gatehouse and crossed the ditch with Kendra helping me along the track and we didn't stop until we were a long way from what had been my home. I was silent, thinking of Oswold's words, and the pain in my heart wouldn't go away. They had called my father a coward, when he was strong and brave, but he hadn't returned to the settlement, and I feared Oswold right and my father must be dead.

ELEVEN

Widsith the Minstrel

I didn't speak until we were back at the Bamburgh road, and Kendra never grumbled about the waste of time or putting her life in danger and I was grateful to her. She said very little, just telling me we must find shelter before dark, but we could see no houses or settlements, only the Bamburgh fortress, high on its rock.

Once, she stopped to drink from a stream trickling through tussocks of grass, but most of the time she hurried me on, and I was too tired and miserable to eat the ripe blackberries and hazel nuts along the way. We trudged beside the heath and the wind blew sand from the dunes across the road and whipped the sea into mountainous waves.

The fortress was closer now and I hoped my father was sitting in the Great Hall, drinking the wine cup with the king. Then remembering Oswold's words, I must have looked sad, for Kendra asked me what was wrong, and I told her about Oswold who'd said my father was dead.

'Don't be daft, you're stupid to listen to a spiteful boy's tale – thought you had more sense,' she said, giving me a push, and I felt more cheerful and imagined King Aethelred listening to my father and banishing Uhtred from his kingdom for ever.

With these happier thoughts, I patted my tunic, found the book safe, and then cursed myself for a fool. I'd taken the monks' precious book with me to my settlement, and Heolstor might have killed me, torn the jewels from the cover, and thrown the book in the ditch. Shuddering with the thought of it, I saw two ragged-looking men coming down the road towards us.

'Do you think they are robbers?' I asked Kendra. 'I don't like the look of them.'

Walking with our heads down and trying not to look at them, we hoped they would go on their way, but they shuffled to a halt in front of us, grinning first at me, then at Kendra, and then at each other.

'What have we here?' said a thin man with a faded red hood and the look of a vicious wolf. He was head and shoulders taller than his fat companion with the wagging belly. He rested his dirty hand on the hilt of the knife stuck in his belt and I smelled sour ale when he leaned towards me.

His small friend, a round headed creature, was pock-faced with one lazy eyelid that made him look as though he winked. His toes were pushing through the holes in his boots and the bindings on his leggings were coming undone. He stretched out one grimy hand with blackened fingernails and pulled at my embroidered cloak and I stepped back, snatching it away from him.

Kendra was quietly watching, but I sensed she was tense and ready to fight. The tall man grinned, looking at his small companion and laughing and showing a mouth full of broken, blackened teeth. 'A bear cub,' he said, the words slurred with too much ale. 'A young bear,' he hiccupped. 'It's a brave cub seeing how his legs don't seem to work. I think he's hiding something under that embroidered cloak. Come from a rich family does he, this bear cub? What do you think, Drogo?'

'No, I don't,' I said. 'No one is rich in these parts, with Eorl Uhtred destroying the villages and taking all we have.'

'Don't you believe him, Ivar,' the small man Drogo said.

They turned to each other and began to dance about the road like clumsy children. Laughing wildly at the game of catch they were inventing for their own amusement, I noticed they watched to see what I would do and I whispered to Kendra to be careful.

The small man Drogo was so fat he soon tired of the dance and ran tottering towards me, but Kendra stuck out her foot and tripped him. He hit the road with a smack, rolled over, and fell with a splash into a ditch. His tall friend Ivar gave a growl and stumbled towards me, a knife clutched in his hand.

'Look out,' screamed Kendra.

Fumbling for father's knife, I backed away and fell over Drogo crawling from the ditch. Covered with waterweed, he threw himself on top of me and bit me on the neck, but most of his teeth were gone and it wasn't painful, just wet, and stinking. Before Kendra could reach me, Ivar rushed forward. Trying to pull his friend to his feet, and stabbing at me with his knife, he was clumsy from drinking too much ale and the blade went into Drogo's arm.

The fat man gave a yell, looking in astonishment at his arm, and Ivar backed away, horrified at what he'd done. Kendra quickly pulled the knife from the pock-faced creature's arm so that he yelped again, and threw it in the bushes. Then snatching her own knife from her belt, she turned to face Ivar. I thrust Drogo off me, he sat up with blood dripping from his arm, and careful to keep out of Ivar's reach, Kendra helped me to my feet.

'There's someone coming,' said Drogo, using the binding from his dirty wet leggings to tie up his wound.

Kendra watched Ivar, keeping him at a safe distance with her knife. 'Sounds like a pilgrim singing,' she said, not turning her head.

'Maybe lepers,' Drogo said mournfully. 'I can hear a bell.'

A man was coming down the road from Lindisfarne pushing a creaking cart, and I heard cheerful singing and the soft tinkling of bells.

'Lepers,' yelled Drogo fearfully, and took to his heels, staggering across the heath towards the forest.

'Off you go, run after him.' Kendra laughed, waving her knife at Ivar's belly, and he cursed her and stumbled after his friend.

The tinkling of bells grew louder, but the man coming towards us had no black leper hood or rags. He wore a startling tunic dyed with woad, and yellow trousers embroidered with moons and stars. On his head was a woollen fool's hat in many colours, its bells jingling as he strode along, and he sang cheerfully as he pushed a handcart painted with poppies.

He stopped and we saw a broad weather-tanned face beaming at us, and he looked from Kendra, who held her knife and was laughing still, and then at Drogo's blood, smeared on my hand. 'I won't ask if that is your blood,' he said to me, 'for your friend with the knife seems too cheerful to have attacked you. Perhaps you would share the cause of so much fun. I'm on my way to Bamburgh, which way do you travel? When I saw you, one was pointing north and the other south.'

Sliding her knife back into her belt and recovering from her giggling, Kendra told him about the robbers and said we were going to Bamburgh village to ask how to find the town of Durham.

'I'm to entertain at the feast at Bamburgh fortress tonight, close by the village,' he said, 'so you will be safer if we travel the road together.' Picking up the handles of the heavily laden cart as if it weighed little, he pushed it along the road with Kendra chatting to him in her strange language, and he seemed to understand her. I hobbled along and felt glad to have the company of a man who was so cheerful and sang so lustily and did not seem afraid of robbers.

I told him our names, and when I asked him about himself, he rested the cart on the road and said, 'Storyteller, singer of songs, juggler, acrobat, minstrel, and fool. The name's Widsith.' Then he bowed solemnly and swept off his hat and the little bells jingled louder than ever.

'What's in the cart, Widsith?' I asked, pointing to the oiled skin cover, my curiosity finally getting the better of me.

'Hats and tunics and shoes for all occasions. There's my harp,

103

things for juggling, and a rope I use to walk high above the heads of those I entertain, whether in fortress or rich man's hall. I sing of battles bravely fought, of treachery, and the famous deeds of kings – why are you going to Durham?' he said.

'We're – we're going with a message to the monks at the White Church. The monastery was attacked and many of the monks were murdered,' I said sadly. I thought of the young monk washed out to sea and shuddered, wondering if I could trust this man and tell him about the holy book I carried.

As we trudged along, Widsith told us funny stories about juggling acts that went wrong. About the time he trained some pigeons to entertain the guests and the cook roasted them by mistake, and about the king's Great Hall at Bamburgh, and listening to his tales, the journey to the fortress did not feel so wearisome. I was more hopeful about finding my father, and Kendra whistled for Modig and he bounded from the heath looking silly with feathers about his mouth and made me laugh.

Thinking we'd reach Bamburgh village before dark, I limped along as cheerfully as I could, but towards evening, the cold wind blew more fiercely from the sea, making it hard for me to keep up with the others. Kendra chatted to Widsith and I was feeling exhausted and annoyed at her for being so cheerful. Wishing she would stop her gossiping that I couldn't understand, and angry with her for taking no notice of me, I heard Widsith call above the wind and saw him pointing to something further down the road.

'The village of Bamburgh,' he shouted, and I could just make out the shapes of thatched houses at the edge of the sea. 'You'd best come to the fortress – you'll not find anyone willing to guide you to Durham this night. I'll tell the guards you're with me and are jugglers come to entertain.'

'We could put bells on Modig,' Kendra shouted back, and her dog growled and slunk beneath the cart.

We entered the village, and protected a little from the gale that threatened to push me over, I looked enviously at candles glowing from behind the oiled skins at the window spaces, where people were warm and safe. Then the short walk through the village ended too soon, and leaving the shelter of the houses the violence of the wind struck again.

In front of us was the outcrop rising sheer sided from the raging sea and towering menacingly above us, and I looked up in the rapidly fading light and shuddered to see the fortress with its palisade like a hideous crown of sharp teeth. There was a steep track from the road to the top of the rock, and Widsith called to Kendra to help him push the cart. I followed them, my leg hurting at every step, and it was only the thought of finding my father in the Great Hall that kept me going.

The higher I went the slower the cart seemed to go, and just when I could climb no further, and must let Widsith and Kendra go on without me, the slope ended and we faced the full fury of the shaking, gusting wind. I could hear the sea pounding and thundering in the darkness below me. My cloak flapped around me and I clung to it, afraid the wind would tear me off the rock, and hurrying after Widsith and Kendra I huddled beside them, protected a little by the gates of the palisade.

Here it was easier to speak, and I watched curiously, as Widsith pulled aside the cover and searched amongst piles of brightly coloured clothing in his cart. Then finding a striped green woollen hood with a long blue tassel, he pulled it on my head and gave me a music pipe made of bone.

'I don't know how to play it,' I protested, giving it back.

'The guests will have drunk so much wine they wouldn't have noticed if you'd squealed it in their ears,' he said, 'but with your embroidered cloak you will do as my assistant. Kendra, we must be rid of your plait, there are few young girls roaming the northern kingdom in the company of a minstrel.'

She wailed almost as loudly as the howling wind when he cut off her plait, and tutting at the fuss she was making, he found a purple hat with a flat crown and floppy yellow brim, and put it on her head. Then hurriedly tucking the straggling bits of her cut hair out of sight, he found bright blue trousers, a woollen tunic, and she reluctantly threw her own clothes into the cart and struggled into her new juggler's outfit.

'Good, now you look splendid,' said Widsith, and he ordered Modig to jump onto the handcart and fastened a red collar with bells around his neck. The dog shook himself, angry at the tinkling noise, and tried to chew them off. The minstrel laughed, and standing close to the iron grille in the gate shouted, 'Widsith with jugglers and a dog to entertain the guests.'

A white face with drink-glazed eyes appeared at the grille, a key turned in a lock, and the small door in the side of the fortress gates opened just enough to allow us through the gap. Then the door banged shut behind us, and Modig leapt from the cart and scampered back to the guard's hut after the smell of food.

'Come here,' Kendra called, but the hound took no notice, angrily shaking his collar.

'He'll do well, probably steal a bone,' Widsith said. 'He's a free spirit like you, Kendra – let's be out of this weather!'

We followed Widsith and the rattling cart down narrow alleyways between empty workshops and passed a forge that reminded me of my father's at home, but the fire was cold. There were few people about, and those we saw hurried passed with heads down, anxious like us to find shelter. Then we turned a corner into a courtyard, and I saw two fine stone buildings. The wind was buffeting against their walls, and they were more magnificent than the church the monks had built on Lindisfarne.

'That's the king's hall where we shall entertain the guests, and the small round building beside it is the king's chapel,' Widsith said. 'The wooden building close to the hall is the kitchen.'

I was glad to see the great oak doors of the hall, but to my dismay, we didn't enter, and following the minstrel wearily around the corner of the building, he stopped at a small side door and knocked. A helmeted guard peered at us through a grille and seeing Widsith let us in. Stumbling over the step, I hurried after the others and the sound of the creaking cart along a dark stone corridor, and coming from the gloom into candle light, found I was in the Great Hall.

I gasped at the size of it, the flagged floor seemed to go on forever, and the roof soared far above me, hidden in darkness. Embroidered tapestries in bright colours hung against the walls and stirred in the draughts, and at the end of the long hall was a raised oak platform. It had a canopy of fine cloth, embroidered with birds and flowers, and beneath it was a table covered with linen, stitched with the picture of a fierce boar's head.

'Who sits there?' I asked Widsith in amazement.

'The king with the important men of the realm. Their women are not allowed to sit with them, but they serve the wine.'

'Look at the fire,' I said, pointing to the stone slabs in the middle of the hall. Logs the thickness of a tree burned brightly, giving off a great heat. There were two long tables down the length of the hall with many candles and covered with costly linen. Rushes dipped in animal fat burned in brackets on the walls, giving off a smoky light, and behind us were steps leading up to the great doors.

Widsith pulled aside a heavy tapestry and pushed the cart into a small alcove beside brooms and buckets. Then Kendra helped him unload the cart, and she picked up some wooden balls and tried to juggle. I watched impatiently, longing to search for my father, and when she seemed to have forgotten me, and was busy chatting with

Widsith, I took off my hood and crept back into the hall.

Seeing a man putting more logs onto the fire, I hurried over to him, tapped him on the arm, and said, 'Have you seen my father? His name's Godwin. He came to see the king.'

'How should I know,' the man replied. 'I don't know any Godwin. Go away, I'm busy.'

'Asking the servants will do you no good,' a cold, dead sounding voice said, and I shuddered and felt sick at the sound of it. 'You'll never see your father again.'

TWELVE

Trapped in the Dungeons

I spun round and saw the hatred in Eorl Uhtred's dark eyes. He no longer wore his chain mail shirt. In its place was a fine linen tunic and a golden torque was at his throat. A boar's head ring glinted in the candlelight, and around his shoulders was the magnificent pelt of a bear.

'I see by your daring you're Godwin's cur, but you are just as stupid as your father,' he said, his voice as cold as ice. Calling to the guards by the great doors of the hall, he shouted, 'Fools! Were you sleeping your duty away? This creature came from behind the tapestry. See if anyone else hides there!'

Two men ran down the steps, hurriedly pulling aside the hangings, and from the alcove, several coloured wooden balls clattered to the floor. They rolled across the paving with Kendra chasing them, and Widsith walked slowly after her into the hall.

'What are you doing skulking in the shadows?' Uhtred demanded, surprised by the minstrel's colourful clothing and his jingling cap.

'Widsith the bard and his juggler, preparing for this evening's entertainment, but as you see, my assistant needs much practice,' Widsith said dryly. Bowing very low, he stared hard at Kendra until she bowed too.

'I know who you are! Do whatever you have to do, and get out of here! We have no need of you yet. Be off to the kitchen where you will be fed,' Uhtred said angrily. Then taking no more notice of Widsith as he hurried Kendra from the hall, he thrust me towards the guards. 'Take him to the dungeons,' he ordered. 'I'll hang him in the morning.'

The men were about to obey his orders, when Uhtred changed his mind and looking at me venomously said, 'Before you enjoy my dungeons, I shall first save you the trouble of worrying about your father. He is dead, slain on the field of battle beside King Aethelred. See, I wear the king's ring. It is a great pity you and the blacksmith will not be there to see me crowned tomorrow.'

'No! You lie! It's not true!' I shouted. Wild with misery, I pulled my knife from its leather case and tried to lunge at him, but a guard caught my wrist, bending back my arm so fiercely I yelled and the knife clattered on the flagstones.

'Pity,' Uhtred said. 'You're too late for this day's hangings.' He gave a short laugh. 'Guards, search the fire brand and make sure he carries no other weapon – then imprison him.'

Uhtred walked away and one guard held my wrists behind my back while the other roughly searched me. The holy book fell from my tunic, tumbled to the floor, and I gave a despairing cry. The jewelled cover shone in the firelight and as the men stared at it in amazement Uhtred turned, saw the book at my feet, and ran to snatch it up.

'Give it back to me,' I shouted, fighting with all my strength to break free from the guards, 'it's Cuthbert's holy book – it doesn't belong to you!'

'My mother's precious necklace,' Uhtred said with his pale face flushed and he was lovingly stroking the cover. 'So this is what happened to it! I wonder how this came into *your* possession.'

'It is a special copy, made for Saint Cuthbert. I'm taking it to the White Church at Durham. I made a solemn promise!'

'The book may be in memory of Cuthbert,' the Eorl said, 'but the jewels are mine. I'm afraid you will not be able to keep your promise. I have had more than enough of your company. Guards, make sure he hangs in the morning.'

The men dragged me across the paving, and I saw Uhtred running up a flight of stairs to a gallery high above the hall. Then I heard a door slam shut and could do nothing to save the book or stop the guards forcing me back through the corridor and out into the courtyard.

I looked desperately about, but there was no sign of Widsith and Kendra, and I felt terribly alone and afraid. Hauling me passed the king's chapel the guards took me to a narrow entrance hewn into the rock with icy walls dimly lit with rushes. Pushed and pulled to the bottom of a steep flight of steps, I saw a paved stone floor and ahead of me a thick oak door with an iron grille.

The gaoler, an old man in sweat smelling rags, sitting on a stool before the door, climbed stiffly to his feet and fumbled with a large iron key ring. Then finding a key that fitted, turned it in the lock. The door swung open, he gave me a push, and I fell, banging my head on the stone floor. Leaning over me, he forced me to sit up, struggled with two iron shackles attached by heavy chains to the wall, and locked them round my ankles. Then shuffling away, and grumbling his food was late, I heard the guards cursing and laughing at him, the sound of their feet scraping on the roughly hewn steps, and a key turning in the dungeon door.

In the faint light from rushes in a bracket on the wall, I peered into the darkest corners of that stinking hole and saw the place empty except for my miserable self. Sitting on fetid straw soaking into my clothes, I listened fearfully to rats scuttling about and wondered if they would attack me. Then I cursed myself for a fool, for why should I worry about rats when the morning would bring a hanging!

Huddled against the wall, I was horrified to see the rushes almost burned away. It would be horrible to spend my last hours with the rats in darkness. Thoughts of mother and Rinan and my grandmother came into my head, and I tried not to think of father dead on the battlefield.

I'd failed the monks and the hermit and the misery of it made me gasp aloud. Numb with cold I wondered fearfully if the morning was creeping nearer. The rushes flickered and were almost out, and I thought about Rinan and hoped he would grow big and strong to look after mother and grandmother. Then I imagined him caring for them better than me, and realised I had been jealous of my brother all my life. He could run and jump, do all the things I never could, and it was my jealousy made me scold him. I felt unbearably sad, for I would never be able to tell him I was sorry.

Lost in these terrible thoughts, and watching the last of the rush light flickering, I heard a noise on the stairs and looked nervously through the bars at the top of the door. For a moment, I couldn't believe what I saw and was too afraid to hope, but it *was* Kendra coming down the steps – she wasn't going to leave me there to die!

She was muttering angrily to herself and I hadn't recognised her at first for she was wearing a stained apron over a gown and a mantle covered her chopped off hair. She was carrying a tray with a large jug, a cup, and something on a plate. Balancing the tray with difficulty she trod carefully, for the gown was too long for her.

Reaching the foot of the steps, I couldn't see her, but I heard her speak to the gaoler and there was the sound of liquid pouring from the jug and the smell of cooked meat. Then to my great distress, she hurried back up the stairs, but I dared not call after her, afraid the gaoler might guess she was there to help me and throw her in prison too.

I sat for a long time, hoping and hoping she would come back, but after a long weary wait, I was beginning to despair. Thinking it must be nearly morning I heard footsteps again and froze in terror. Watching the stairs, and expecting the guards to drag me from the dungeons, my fear turned to wild hope and I had to stop myself from shouting out – it was Kendra!

I heard a rattling noise and the door swung open, and she held the gaoler's bunch of keys. Kneeling beside me, she quickly grabbed at the shackles around my ankles, pushing one key after another into the locks and cursing softly, for she could find none to fit.

'Where's the gaoler?' I whispered nervously.

'When I brought food from the kitchen Widsith put something in his ale, but I don't know how long it will…. it's useless!' She shook the shackles savagely as though she would break them open with her fists. 'I can't find the right key!'

I looked up at her miserably, expecting the gaoler to wake and catch her. She scrambled to her feet and for one terrible moment, I thought she was leaving me. I caught at her gown, but furiously shaking her head she reached up to the spluttering rushes and scraped the last of the melted fat from the iron bracket with her fingers. Then crouching beside me, she pulled off my boots without undoing the strings and rubbed the still warm fat over my feet and under the shackles as far as she could reach.

'This should do it,' she muttered to herself, 'he's thin enough.' She pulled at one of the shackles, squeezing my heel so much it was hard not to cry out. Then with a tremendous tug, my foot slipped free.

Kendra fell back on the straw and the iron chain rattled on the stone floor. We froze, hardly daring to breathe. We waited, but no sound came from the gaoler, and Kendra urgently pulled at the other shackle around my bad leg with all her strength.

This time it was easy, for the leg was thinner and the iron band slipped off. Shoving my boots back on, she pulled me to my feet. I was so cold and stiff I could hardly move, but ignoring the hurt in my body, I hobbled after her as fast as I could. The gaoler was slumped on the floor, the empty jug and a half gnawed meat bone beside him. Terrified he might wake, I climbed the steps as fast as my leg would let me with Kendra helping me to the top.

Then telling me to wait, she disappeared into the courtyard. Returning moments later she said, 'There's drunken laughter and singing from the hall. Rain is bouncing off the paving, so I don't think we need worry about the guards. If they've any sense, they'll be inside keeping dry. It's safe if we're quick. Come on.'

'Which way?' I asked, the rain beating in my face as I followed her out into the courtyard.

'To the gate house. Widsith said he'd meet us there with Modig. He'll tell the guards the entertainment is over and he'll bring us through the gates.'

She beckoned me to follow, and splashing through the puddles I kept close to the wall of the king's chapel. I was trying not to be left behind, and miserably rubbing the rain from my eyes with my sleeve, when I noticed strange animals and birds, like those in the monk's holy book, carved deep into the large stone cross above the chapel door.

'What are you stopping for?' Kendra called, coming back to seize at my arm. 'Come on! Widsith could be waiting by the gate! Unless you intend to stay here and drown,' she shouted.

'I can't, I can't leave without the holy book!'

'This is madness – you'll never find it. You don't know where it is.

Let's get away from here before they hang us both,' she said angrily.

'I *do* know where to find it!' I pushed her away and pointed through the rain to an outside flight of steps from the courtyard to the upper floor of the king's hall. 'There's a door at the top - I think it leads to the upstairs room where Uhtred sleeps!'

'He may have the book with him!' Kendra said angrily, but I was already limping away from her.

Climbing up the stone steps, the gale was so violent I had to cling to crevices in the wall to stop it hurling me to the paving below. Kendra followed me, tripping over her gown and shouting for me to come back. Reaching the top of the stairs, I thought I heard a man bellowing at me from below. Not daring to look down, I opened the door, and shouting at Kendra to hurry, and bundling her ahead of me, I closed it behind us as fast as I could.

Within the thick stone walls the sound of the thumping, moaning wind was less, and I heard wild laughter drifting up from the hall below and knew I was right. We were in the long gallery, near the top of the staircase I'd seen Uhtred climb when the guards dragged me to the dungeons.

'Follow me,' I whispered, but I needn't have bothered about anyone hearing us, for the drunken revelry in the hall below, and the wind tearing round the walls, and wailing like a vengeful ghost, hid any noise of our footsteps. Keeping as close to the back wall as I could and hoping no one would look up between the pillars and see me, I crept towards a heavy oak door at the end of the gallery. Then beckoning Kendra to follow me, I carefully pushed it open.

The room was full of frightening shadows, the sound of the sea crashing on the rocks boomed around us, seeming to shake the walls. Candles spluttered wax in the draughts seeping through gaps in the shutters over the window places, their thin light darting over walls and ceiling, and a huge bed, with a black bear's pelt for a cover, almost filled the room.

'It's cold in here and I hate the sound of an angry sea,' said Kendra, shivering in her wet gown. 'Hurry up and find that book before someone finds *us*!'

I looked around, wondering where to start searching, and saw an animal with great tusks snarling at me from the shadows and backing away knocked into Kendra.

'Stop it,' she muttered, 'it's only a boar's head nailed to the piece of wood, and it won't get you!'

'This must be the king's room – my father says he wears a ring with a boar's head. Now Uhtred has it on his finger,' I said bitterly.

'Never mind that,' hissed Kendra, 'Widsith has probably given up and left without us, and it'll be your fault. Let's find the book and leave!' She lifted the lid of a chest, pulling out clothes and dropping them on the floor around her. I searched on the table beside the bed and cried, 'Kendra – look at this!'

'What is it? Have you found it?'

I held up a thin gold frame that held a small painting of a woman with dark hair and a long pale face. 'The woman in the painting – she

118

looks like Uhtred,' I said.

'Must be his mother,' said Kendra.

'Look at the necklace she's wearing – those are the jewels on the cover of the gospels. So Uhtred is right, they did belong to his mother Juliana!'

'We came to find the book,' Kendra said, trying to see what I'd discovered. Then hearing me gasp she said crossly, 'Now what have you found? It's only some torn old book.'

'No it isn't, it's the gospels!' I said miserably, pointing to the paintings of winged animals with claws and the fat legged birds with enormous eyes. 'It's Cuthbert's book, but the cover's ripped off! The jewels are gone and Uhtred must have–'

'Be quiet! I heard something!' Kendra warned.

I snatched up the torn book, stuffing it inside my tunic, and opened the door with shaking hands. I could hear shouting from the guests below, but there was no one in the gallery. Still tingling with fear, I beckoned Kendra to follow me, hurried as fast as I could to the door at the end of the corridor, and found it locked.

'We can't get out,' I whispered, but Kendra was already creeping down the stairs to the hall, and terrified someone would look up and see me, I followed her.

At the foot of the steps, I found her crouching in a narrow gap between the tables and the wall, half hidden by tapestries, and I squatted beside her. Guests on the benches had their backs to us, but they were horribly close. Through smoke drifting from the burning logs, and the light from smouldering torches, I saw Uhtred seated at the high table. On both sides of the Eorl were strange warriors with hats of fur and the pelts of bears around their shoulders, and I thought they must be the huscarls from across the seas.

Then suddenly the drunken noise in the hall was hushed and looking nervously around for the reason, I saw Widsith walk slowly down the hall, a small, many-stringed harp in his arms. He bowed low to Uhtred, and standing close to the high table he began to play, the guests watching in silence as his long fingers caressed the strings.

Strange plaintive music quivered in the air, spreading like circles in a clear pool, enticing the guests into a dreaming spell. His voice, soft and low, drew his listeners to him, and in the magic of his words the tapestries lifted, the hall was gone, and the night sky was above me. I was wandering on a mist-covered heath where a savage battle raged and heard the clash of swords and the dull clang of hammer on shield.

Men fought with spear and axe, in the bitter struggle ground was lost and won many times, and it was hard to tell which army would be the victor. Then a big man with hair and beard the colour of straw rallied those around him and my heart leapt at the sight of him.

Brandishing his axe, and with fierce cries he led the charge, giving many ringing blows to left and right and fighting valiantly. Being the first to break the shield-wall, others followed him through the gap of fallen men, and the defeated shield bearers, carrying the banners of Mercia, threw down their weapons, ran from the heath, and deserted their fallen.

Raucous shouts rang out and a host of victorious men, proudly wearing the boar's head tunics, gathered round to cheer their Northumbrian king. I called to my father, and hurrying across the heath, I tried to reach him, but the men were dissolving like mist around me and my hands went through them as I touched them. Crying out and begging them to stay, they drifted away from me into the night, the sound of their rejoicing fading to a murmur, and the sights conjured by the bard were gone.

The harp fell silent and the spell was broken. The Eorl was staring at Widsith, white faced and fearful, and the guests shook themselves, as if rising from a deep slumber. Looking startled for a moment, they seized the nearest cup and drank deeply, and the hall filled with the noise of fists banging on tables for the servants to bring more food and wine.

Waking from my strange dream, and bitterly disappointed not to have found my father, I felt Kendra nudge me and she muttered in my ear, 'Quick – in this noise they'll never notice us. If we can reach the end of the tables we might be able to get to the doors before we're caught!' Beckoning me to follow her, she crawled rapidly across the paving, lifted the edge of a tablecloth, and disappeared.

Alarmed, I scuttled after her under the table, and crawling through a tunnel of legs, heard an angry bellow and the fearful words, 'The prisoner has escaped, the prisoner has escaped!'

Uhtred yelled at the guards to search the hall and Kendra was moving so fast it was hard to keep up with her. I'd nearly reached the end of the tables, and desperate to know how far we were from the doors, I saw the linen cloth move and the surprised upside-down face of the gaoler looking at me. Giving a roar of anger, he grabbed me by my cloak and dragged me into the hall, one guard pulled Kendra after me, and she shrieked, kicking and fighting to break free.

Uhtred strode towards me, his face dark with anger, and shook me violently. 'I thought I was rid of you,' he cried, 'but now I see you have returned with a wild bedraggled creature that looks like one of my slaves!' He turned to the gaoler and with the venom of a grass snake said, 'Make sure they don't escape – unless you want to hang beside them in the morning!'

The guards dragged Kendra away, and clawing like a wild mountain cat, she screamed Widsith's name. Throwing down his harp, the minstrel leapt over the tables and ran swiftly down the hall. Seizing the surprised Eorl by the neck, he pulled him off balance, backing with him against the wall and using him as a shield, and I was astonished to see Widsith held my father's knife at Uhtred's throat, just above the golden torque.

'What interest do you have in these poor wretches, Widsith?' Uhtred sneered, struggling to break free from the minstrel's grip. 'Surely, you could find hundreds like them, willing to serve you? Don't lose your life for such a useless cause. Return to your playing or my men will disarm you and you'll dance on the gallows at first light, together with your *very* strange friends.'

'Let the boy and girl free,' Widsith shouted, but the guards and

122

gaoler hesitated. The minstrel pressed father's hunting knife against Uhtred's neck, scoring his skin and drawing blood. The Eorl screeched in terror, and the guards released us.

'Run,' shouted Widsith, and Kendra took my hand and pulled me towards the steps to the doors of the great hall. The huscarls drew their swords, moving towards Widsith, and I heard Uhtred scream at them to kill the minstrel.

THIRTEEN

The Return of the King

Kendra tugged me up the steps from the hall, and we'd almost reached the top when I heard the clatter of hooves and the great doors burst open. Wind brought rain sweeping into the hall, and through the doorway, I saw battle weary thegns dismounting from mired horses with royal trappings and one man held high the boar's head banner of the King of Northumbria.

Kendra and I shuffled against the wall and warriors in mud-spattered chain mail marched down the steps into the Great Hall. Their eyes glinted through the facemasks of their rusted iron helmets. The once bright colours of Aethelred on shield and tunic were faded, and the shields axe-scarred and split, but these men were a powerful and brave sight.

I'd seen such warriors riding the Bamburgh road on the king's business, but I had never been so close. Their battle stench was sour as they passed me. Heavy axes hung from their broad leather belts, and the tips of their double-edged swords struck sparks on the flagstones.

The huscarls dropped their weapons clattering to the paving, and they came to kneel before the grey haired warrior at the foot of the steps. There were shocked murmurs from the guests and I heard the word Aethelred and knew the old man with the wide chest of the bear must be the king.

His men formed a line along the hall, their chain mail clinking, and I noticed someone standing next to the king and my heart filled with joy. Although his cloak was filthy, and his tangled straw-coloured beard and hair were matted, it was my father Godwin. There was a livid scar running from his forehead into his beard. He looked tired and older, but it was still my father, and I wanted to push my way through the warriors crowded on the steps and like Rinan, run and hug him.

Widsith took my father's knife from Uhtred's throat and walked slowly to the king, but the Eorl pushed passed him, saying boldly, 'My lord, we were brought news you were killed, had died in battle,' and he knelt before Aethelred.

Then the deep voice of the king rang through his hall. 'Get to your feet, traitor, you took a solemn vow you would care for the kingdom in my absence and protect my people. Instead you have robbed and murdered, burning down villages when my loyal people dared to stand against you!'

White faced, Uhtred jumped up, pointed to my father, and shouted, 'There is your traitor – he and his men rose against you – refused to pay your lawful taxes.'

'You were collecting taxes for your own money chests, nephew. I've seen for myself the villages you have destroyed and the homeless you have left in your wake. I trusted you, and yet you tricked others into thinking me dead. Now you wear one of my rings, hold a feast, and plan to wear my crown!'

'Mercy, my Lord, I beg pardon– '

'Enough,' the king thundered. 'I will deal with you later. For your mother's sake, I shall be more lenient than you would have been with me, had I been at your mercy. First, I must know what was happening when I came into my hall. I find the most famous minstrel in my land with a knife at your throat and surrounded by huscarls ready to cut him down!'

Widsith stepped forward and bowed low. 'I come from Lindisfarne and bring bad news. Northmen have attacked the monastery and the monks slain. The holy treasure is stolen, but the boy accompanying me is Toland, son of Godwin, sworn to guard the gospels of Lindisfarne with his life and bring the book safe to the White Church in Durham.'

'Where is this boy?' the king asked.

I climbed awkwardly down the steps, astonished at the minstrel's words. The thegns made way for me and I tried to kneel before the king, but I was so tired it was hard to do and Widsith caught me by the elbow and bade me stand.

'A boy who hobbles was given this task, Widsith?' the king said in surprise.

'He is Godwin's son, and although his body is weak, he is loyal and brave when need be. He saw his family safe with the nuns at Ancroft, although Uhtred tried to murder him and his kinsfolk too.'

'Are the gospels with you now?' the king asked me.

'I have only a part,' I said, feeling flustered, for all were listening, but my father looked at me with great kindness. 'The jewelled cover is missing – Uhtred tore it from the holy book.'

'Search the Eorl Uhtred,' the king ordered.

Two men held Uhtred fast and he fought like a wild beast, but they ripped the scrip from his waist and removed the book's cover. One man gave it to the king, and those near enough to see the gold and silver cross on it, and the many garnets and amethysts glinting in the firelight, stared in amazement.

'Uhtred, these precious gemstones were given to the monks in payment for your father's blood debt,' Aethelred said, angrily.

'The jewels do not belong to the monks,' the Eorl said, his voice icy and intent on his bitter words. 'They were part of my mother Juliana's golden necklace, given to her by my grandfather on her wedding day. My father had no right to take her gift. She promised it to me when she was dying as the last token of her love.'

'Rightly or wrongly it was given to the monks of Lindisfarne where they put it to good use,' said Aethelred. 'Your Father murdered my brother, and would have murdered me to take my place, as you had planned to do. His blood debt was great and he gave the necklace to the monks as payment for a terrible wrong.'

'No, the necklace was stolen - stolen goods can never pay a blood debt,' Uhtred said defiantly. 'Those jewels are mine.' Breaking free from the guards, he leapt forward, snatched the cover from the king's hands, and sprang onto the table, knocking over wine cups and sending them clattering and rolling across the paving.

He ran along the tables, red wine dripping from them like blood. The guards and many of the thegns chased after him, some waiting to trap him at the end of the hall. Uhtred looked frantically about him but could see nowhere to escape. One warrior made a grab for his legs, but the Eorl leapt up to a window ledge, clinging to the tapestry and pushing the cover of the holy book inside his tunic. A guard jumped onto the table and tried to reach him, but Uhtred kicked out wildly, swinging on the tapestry to avoid capture, and collided with the shutters with a terrible crash.

There was a wild cry, the wind gusted through the empty window space, and the broken shutters creaked and clattered against the wall. All stood in shocked silence, looking to where he had been, and I shuddered to think of him falling and his body dashed violently on the rocks below.

'A pity,' the king sighed, his voice rising about the wind and the crashing of the waves against the rock, 'but he has saved me the trouble of hanging him. It is a blessing his mother Juliana is not here to see this day.' Then noticing me still standing before him, he said, 'Godwin, is this your son?'

'Yes,' my father said, bowing to the king.

'I think he will serve me well, as you served Eorl Leof. Later, I shall send for him to join my household. Such loyalty should be rewarded.' Then looking at me, he said quietly, 'You have Cuthbert's holy book?'

128

I pulled the book from my tunic and held it out and Aethelred took it from me carefully, running his fingers over the damaged spine. 'It is sad to find the gospels, copied especially in honour of Cuthbert, in such a sorry state. What think you, Widsith?'

'The words of the four gospels are more precious than any jewel. It is good that the monks used such skill to make a magnificent cover, but those words need no jewels to make them worthy. No, the book is better far without precious stones given in payment for a blood debt,' the minstrel said.

'I promised to carry the holy book to Durham,' I said, anxious to see the king hold the book so long and afraid he might not return the gospels to me.

'Do you wish to keep your promise and take Cuthbert's book to Durham?' the king asked me. 'I think your father would prefer you came home with him to your family. You have had enough adventuring. I shall send one of my messengers to carry it to the White Church.'

'No!' I said in alarm, secretly ashamed I had failed the monks before and now determined to keep my promise. 'My word is given – I vowed to take the holy book to the monks at Durham.'

I thought my father looked angry at my outburst, but the king laughed. 'He is indeed your son, Godwin, you should be proud of him. He shall have food, and then you may take him away and see he has everything for his journey. I shall send a messenger with him to keep him safe on the road.'

My father kissed the king's hand and I heard Aethelred promise that he would forever be our hearth lord and protect us from the Northmen. Then the king sent the guests from the hall, and seated with my father and the thegns, Kendra and I stuffed as much of the left-over pies, cold mutton, pork, game fowl, and sweetmeats into our mouths as we could reach.

I tasted the wine and found it bitter, and Kendra spat it out. Between mouthfuls, I told father all that had happened and that our family was safe. 'Siward saved our lives and did not give us away, even when Uhtred threatened to hang him,' I exclaimed, spraying crumbs everywhere. 'He led mother, Rinan, and grandmother to the nuns at Ancroft.' Then I thought for a moment and said, 'Uhtred knew I was with my family in the forest. Heolstor said he told the Eorl where to find us, wanting to save his kinsfolk, but Uhtred did not keep his word. When his dogs did not pick up our scent, he returned and destroyed our settlement.'

'I will speak with my brother,' my father said quietly. 'I believe he betrayed you to save his own skin, but enough of that at present, is there anything else I should know?'

'Now the king has given me permission to take the holy book to the White Church, I shall not go without Kendra.'

'Has Kendra been given her freedom?'

'It doesn't matter,' I said, for the little wine I'd drunk had made me reckless. 'The abbot who owned her is dead, Kendra belongs only to herself,' and hearing my words, Kendra grinned at me and crammed more pastries into her mouth.

After a rested night, with no horrible dreams, I woke early from my bed of reeds on the hall floor. Wondering where I was, and pulling on my cloak that had served me as bed cover, I crept passed the servants asleep on benches, along the corridor to the side door, and into the courtyard. I was hoping to find Widsith, and ask how he knew I carried the holy book, but Kendra was waiting for me with Modig at her feet. She was dressed once more in her old tunic and trousers, and someone had trimmed her poor hair where Widsith had cut off her plait.

'Here, he left you this,' she said gruffly, holding out my knife.

'Where did he find it? Has Widsith gone?' I said. 'I wanted to thank him and say good-bye.' Puzzled, I took my knife and felt sad that he'd left without speaking to me, but I did not have long to think about this, for I saw Fugol the king's messenger mounted on a wonderful stallion and leading two ponies across the courtyard towards us.

Reluctantly saying a quick farewell to my father, I heard Kendra grumbling loudly and saying the beasts we must ride were not as good as her father's mountain ponies but they would do. Then making ourselves comfortable in the fine saddles, and waving to my father, we rode after the messenger on his magnificent horse with its trappings embroidered with the boar's head emblem and followed him down the steep slope that brought us onto the road.

As we trotted away from the fortress, the sea glittered in the cold sunlight on the shore and hearing the powerful rushing of the tide, I wondered if the waves had washed Uhtred's body out to sea. These dark thoughts made me shiver, so instead, I imagined my father on his way to the nuns' house to let mother, grandmother, and Rinan know I was safe, and that made me feel better.

Seated on my pony, with the king's messenger riding before me, and Kendra on her pony by my side, I watched Modig trotting along and searching for small creatures in the grasses. He looked happy now he'd finally chewed off his jingling collar, and for the first time for a long while, I began to feel happy too.

The day was fine and a breeze came from the sea, and we were covering the ground at quite a pace. As we rode along, I asked Fugol to tell me the names of places we passed on the way. Being pleasant natured, he was willing to point to the remains of forts where warriors had won or lost famous battles, and passing distant villages, he told me their names and about those who lived there. Wanting to know what his life as a king's messenger was like, he answered my eager questions, and it sounded exciting and I hoped to be like Fugol and ride for the king.

The first day passed pleasantly enough and we came to a village at dusk, stopping at an inn, and Fugol knocked to ask for rooms. The innkeeper saw the king's man with his powerful mount and rich clothing, and promised us food and comfortable beds, but the beds were lumpy and full of fleas.

This kept me wakeful most of the night, scratching and listening to

Fugol snoring beside me. Tossing and turning, I pulled the precious book from under my pillow, and through the open shutters, the moon shone on the swirling shapes and I tried to guess their meaning. Looking at the bright animals, and the birds strutting in the silvery light, I gently traced their outline with my fingers, giving each a name, and fell asleep.

For several days we moved from village to village, then one bright fresh morning, with the dew wet on the grass, we left the inn and climbing into the saddle, trotted to the brow of a hill. From this high point, I gasped at the sight of a vast stretch of land sloping away from me, and saw in the distance the surface of a broad river, glinting as it flowed into the sea.

'Durham at last!' Fugol said, and shading my eyes, I followed the course of the river inland and saw a bridge, a high stone wall surrounding the town, and a hill covered with trees.

The steeply descending road took us through fields of winter wheat, woodland with rooting pigs, and apple orchards, and the sun had climbed well into the sky as we reached the bottom of the hill. Now I could see the grey town walls ahead, and we joined the many people from nearby villages travelling along the road, some on foot, and others pushing carts, and we found it difficult to avoid the rumbling wagons as we rode towards the bridge.

With a sudden feeling of excitement, and wondering what a town would be like, I caught up with Fugol and he pointed to the top of the hill where the white walls of a church tower reflected the morning light. 'That must be what you're looking for – not far now, and you'll have kept your promise,' he said in a kindly way.

Urging our ponies through the crowds, the road narrowed into a muddy lane with many houses and workshops close together. Hardly able to move forward, and seeing an inn, I called to Kendra to dismount and climbed down from the saddle.

'Stable our ponies here, it won't take long to reach the church,' I said to Fugol, for I was eager to see the town and not wanting to take our mounts into such a busy place. 'We shall meet you here.'

'The king said–'

'What harm can it do, Fugol? We'll not be gone long.' Before he could answer, I made sure the holy book was safe in my tunic and hurried after Kendra and Modig.

We saw men driving oxen from the water meadows into the town for slaughter, and we followed a flock of sheep over the bridge and Modig nipped at their heels. Squawking geese pattered by, honking and hissing at the hound, and he ran after them, biting at their tail feathers.

I was enjoying the sights and sounds around me and weaving through the crowds that were shoving and pushing over the bridge, when I realised I couldn't see Kendra. Anxiously trying to find her, someone grabbed me by the neck, dragged me from the bridge, and pulled me down the bank close to the river.

FOURTEEN
At Dudda's Tavern

My arms were held behind my back and a cord tied round my wrists so tight I shouted out with pain. Then the cord was jerked viciously, and tugged beneath one of the arches of the bridge I heard a familiar voice say, 'What have we here?'

Drogo, the little man with an eye that winked on its own, pushed his grinning face close to mine, and from the vile smell, I knew it was Ivar with the red hood pulling on the cord.

'It's the rich bear cub,' Drogo said, poking me in the ribs. 'Saw him at the inn with the king's messenger – must have something on him that's worth our trouble. Not rich at all, so he told us. Now let's see what he's carrying under that cloak.'

He dragged at my belt and pulled the monks' book from my tunic, turning it over in his filthy fingers. Then with a shrug, he was about to throw it in the river when my horrified cry stopped him, and changing his mind, he looked at it with a puzzled frown.

'Seems to want to keep it,' Drogo said to his tall friend who tugged the cord, making me stumble.

'If he wants it then it's worth a bit. What else he's got?' Ivar asked.

Drogo fumbled with my brooch, stabbing his finger with the pin. Cursing he flung back my cloak and was searching me again when I was astonished to see Kendra drop from the bridge and land soundlessly on the grass. Springing forward, she knocked the book from Drogo's hand, thumped him in the belly, and he fell and slid down the bank. Clutching the reeds, and hanging with his feet dangling close to the surface of the fast flowing river, he squealed with fear.

Turning to face Ivar, Kendra watched him, cat-like and ready to see what he'd do. Ivar looked at her in surprise and pulled on the cord, dragging me after him. This time he was sober and dangerous, and he snatched up the book from the bank.

He grinned at Kendra, wrenching my arms up behind my back and I cried out as the cord bit into my wrists. 'Come near and I'll break the cub's arms and the book goes in the river,' he threatened.

'Keep the book, I don't want it, just let my friend go,' she said.

'No,' I shouted, 'save the gospels – forget about me!'

At that moment, Drogo lost his hold on the reeds and let out a loud yell. Falling in the water with a great splash, he sank out of sight.

'Your little friend seems to be drowning,' Kendra said, grinning at Ivar.

There was another loud cry as Drogo bobbed up again, frantically splashing to stay afloat.

'Let my friend go and I'll save the useless lump. You'd best make up your mind, he won't last much longer,' she laughed.

'All right – I'll let the cub go if you pull Drogo from the river, not before!' Ivar said.

A crowd had gathered on the bridge to watch Drogo fighting to reach the bank, and Kendra dived into the water, swimming strongly like a seal towards the drowning man. He snatched at her hair, trying to save himself and she punched him on the jaw to quieten him. Then supporting the half-conscious Drogo under his arms, she swam with him to the bank and pulled his soggy body onto the grass.

'He looks a lot cleaner,' Kendra said, squeezing the water out of her tunic and watching him spluttering and fighting for breath. 'He'll live. Now keep your part of the bargain and let my friend go, or I'll throw him in the river again!'

By this time, the crowd on the bridge had recognised Ivar. Waving their fists at the thief, they ran down the bank to catch him, but he dropped the end of the cord, fled along the path by the river, and disappeared into the trees.

'You shouldn't have done it! You shouldn't have done it! All this way for nothing,' I shouted at Kendra as she untied the cord from my wrists. 'You let Ivar go and he's taken the book!'

'Cheer up. You don't think I'd have let him hurt you, do you? Stop looking like a dog with a bellyache. We'll find him sure enough and get the book back. Or are you going to stand there all day feeling sorry for yourself?'

I trailed after her to the bridge, rubbing my wrists and feeling hopeless. 'We'll never find him,' I said miserably, 'where do we start looking in such a big place?'

She took no notice of me and I followed her along narrow lanes into an old part of the town where houses with rotting thatch and neglected strips of garden were crammed between small workshops along the river.

'Where are we going?' I said, struggling to keep up with her, 'we'll never find Ivar!'

'Stop moaning,' Kendra growled, stopping to face me with her hands on her hips. 'It's me should be doing the complaining. I saved your life, the river was freezing, and my clothes are clinging to me and all you do–'

'Look there's someone over there – let's ask him,' I said hurriedly and pointed to an old man sitting in an open doorway. He had a reed basket at his feet with a few vegetables for sale and an old wicker cage with a thin chicken peering through the bars.

Anxious to get away from Kendra, I hurried over to him saying, 'Have you seen a man with a red hood? He has a small friend with a pockmarked face and a lazy eyelid, and he–'

'You mean cut throat Ivar?' the man said, laughing hoarsely. 'Most people round here know him, but best keep away from him if you have any sense.'

'I must speak to him, it's important.'

'What would the likes of you want with Ivar?' he said. Roughly shaking the cage and making the chicken squawk, he held out one grimy hand. 'What have you got to give me?'

'Don't hurt the chicken!' I said quickly. 'I'll buy it if you tell me where I can find Ivar,' and I offered him a piece of a coin my father had provided for my journey. I knew it would buy many chickens and his eyes widened.

Snatching it from me, he bit it and nodded with satisfaction. 'Ivar spends most of his time with Drogo at Dudda's Tavern, when he's not out on the road robbing. If you ask Dudda, he'll know where to find him. Go down the lane on the left – you'll see the sign over the door. The two of them are usually in there selling what they've stole. Though you'd better not go near them if you want to live long,' he wheezed, struggling for breath.

I picked up the cage and the chicken hopped about, trying to keep its balance. Walking away, he shouted after me, telling me to bring back his cage, but I took no notice.

'What do you want that thing for? It's got hardly any feathers,' Kendra said. 'It won't lay eggs.'

'Don't know, but I'm not leaving it to be treated badly – it's mine, I paid for it.'

'It's not even fit for the pot,' she said, peering at it through the bars. 'There's no meat on it.'

'Well, it's not going to be eaten, I shall take it home, and it can roost with our hens on the beams in our house.'

She shook her head at me, and we turned into a lane full of holes filled with rotted food and dung. Avoiding the bones, fish entrails, and vegetables scraps stinking in heaps before the doors, we came to Dudda's tavern. Through the window space, I saw the small dark room was crowded with men sitting on benches with jugs of ale. A couple had a tafl board on the bench between them and throwing bone dice, and a man with a filthy apron was holding a dirty cloth and straining a cloudy mixture from a bowl into a barrel.

'Don't know why you bother, Dudda, the stuff's only fit for pigs,' one man said.

'Then it will be all right for you,' Dudda grinned, and finished straining the liquid.

Pushing open the door of the evil smelling place, we walked through ale slops on the dirt floor and the customers stared at us suspiciously. Feeling nervous, I went up to the man with long greasy hair called Dudda and said, 'We're looking for Ivar.'

'Not here,' he said, fitting the lid on the barrel. 'What do you want with him?'

'He took something belonging to me,' I said.

'Ivar brings me many things he collects – what might you be looking for?'

'It's a book.'

'It's not worth much,' Kendra added quickly.

'If it's worth nothing, I'm wondering why you come looking for it,' the tavern keeper said. Then ducking his head under the beams he disappeared into a back room, returned with Cuthbert's holy book, and put it down on top of the barrel.

'That's it,' I said, not wanting to sound too eager.

'Well. Are you going to pay me, or not?'

'It was stolen from us,' Kendra said indignantly.

'As maybe,' Dudda said, 'but if I gives it to you, then what am I going to give Ivar? He expects to get something for the trouble he went to, bringing it to me in the first place,' and he placed one wet, ale-stained hand on the gospels.

'I've no money,' I said hurriedly, 'but I have this,' and I held out the chicken in its cage.

The tavern keeper laughed and shook his head. Then in desperation, I tugged my cloak over my head and held it out to Dudda. He fingered the embroidery, then without a word, his hand shot out and he pulled my father's knife from my belt. Removing it from its leather case, he admired the engraving along the blade.

'I'll take this in payment,' he said.

I bit my lip, my heart heavy to see my father's hunting knife in the tavern keeper's hands. Then fearing Dudda might change his mind, I snatched up my cloak, stuffed the gospels inside my tunic, and hurried from the tavern after Kendra.

FIFTEEN

The White Church

Limping down the road, I pushed Cuthbert's book tight inside my tunic and hurrying as fast as I could, followed Kendra into the tightly packed crowds and the noise of the busy market. People were shuffling along the narrow lanes between the booths and carts, and as the crush of bodies carried us along, I felt Kendra dig me in the ribs and saw she held my father's hunting knife in her fist.

'Didn't think you would want to part with it,' she said, with a wicked grin, 'so I took it from Dudda when he wasn't looking. Better be quick before he comes after us,' and before I could thank her, she was lost in the mass of slowly moving people in front of the stalls.

Hooking the knife back onto my belt with a feeling of great relief, and putting on my cloak, I held tight to the chicken's cage and ducked to avoid a peddler's heavy backpack. Then catching sight of Kendra again, and anxious she should not leave me behind, I heard a strange whooshing noise and in a space between two stalls saw a terrifying sight.

A man was puffing flames from his throat like a dragon, thrusting a burning stick into his mouth, and swallowing the fire. I wanted to see if he would set his belly alight, and wriggling between customers crowding round a cart laden with flagons of ale, I nearly fell over an old beggar woman sitting on the ground. Feeling sorry for her, and thinking she looked like grandmother, I thrust the cage with the squawking chicken into her arms and an angry shout made me jump.

The crowds were shuffling away, and a huge black bear was lumbering towards me. It was walking on its hind legs, and it reared up, its head turning and its small eyes wild and dangerous. A squat, bandy-legged man, tugging on the heavy iron chain round the bear's neck, yelled at me to get out of the way.

The animal was so close I could see the thick dust in its coat and the patches of raw flesh on its neck where the chain had rubbed away its coarse dark fur. It lashed out half-heartedly with its paw and I ducked, but another pull on the chain quietened it, and there was a strong leather muzzle fastened round its jaws. I was glad of that, but I felt pity for the creature, for Ivar had tugged me on a cord and I knew what it felt like.

'What will happen to the bear?' I asked Kendra when I managed to catch up with her. 'The poor creature looks tired and ill.'

'He makes it dance,' she said. She'd reached the last of the market stalls and wasn't really listening, and following her towards a path at the foot of the wooded hill, I could see the tower of the White Church, just visible above the trees.

'Come on, do you want to get there before dark or not?' she said.

'Where's the chicken?'

'Someone needed it,' I said quickly.

'Well, it wasn't much good,' she said.

143

There were few people coming up and down the path and Kendra climbed steadily through the wood, sometimes waiting for me to catch up, and sometimes walking on ahead. I looked back several times, thinking someone was following me, but each time the path was empty. Struggling up the hill was exhausting, but as I came out of the trees, a feeling of growing excitement took the place of tiredness.

On level ground at the top of the hill was the church at last, its wooden whitewash covered walls and small bell tower shining in the pale sunlight. A stream was flowing close to the church wall, and hearing a heavy clunking sound, I saw water pouring over the rim of a dam from a side leat and surging along a millrace to turn a rumbling wheel on the side of a mill. Fascinated, I watched the swinging buckets scooping up water, carrying it over the top of the wheel, and emptying it back into the millrace. Then beyond the mill, the stream meandered through reed beds and finally hurried down the hill to the river.

Not far from the church was the monastery, and beside a cluster of smaller buildings was a long wooden house. It reminded me of the one on Lindisfarne with the shuttered windows, and in a small garden, two monks with their robes kilted were hoeing vegetables.

Touching the book in my tunic several times, and making sure it was still there, I looked round for Kendra and saw her sitting on a stone wall in front of the church. I hurried over to her and heard the door of the long house open. A tall monk was walking along the path towards us, his black robes flapping around his bare feet, and I was astonished and pleased to see it was the hermit from Inner Farne. He greeted us warmly, and for a moment his eyes above the reddish beard suddenly reminded me of someone else, then the memory was gone.

'I see you have kept your promise,' he said, noticing me clutching nervously at my tunic. 'You must come with me and meet Abbot Alfric.'

He opened the gate, and we followed him along the pebbled path and through the porch into the peaceful church. It took some time for my eyes to become used to the deeper shadows and to realise a frail, black robed monk, with a pectoral cross of gold and silver, was smiling at Kendra and me as we came near.

'Father Abbot, this is Toland who promised to bring the Lindisfarne Gospels to you, and with him is Kendra, who has helped him on his journey,' the hermit said.

'I received a message from the king to say you were on your way. You must have endured many hardships. I did not think to see the gospels in my lifetime,' the abbot said, and I took the book from my tunic and put it into his transparent, trembling hands.

'At last, Saint Cuthbert's book!' he said softly with tears in his eyes. 'Come, it shall be placed on the altar where it belongs.'

We followed the abbot as he shuffled along the stone-flagged floor and watched him gently lay the book on the altar cloth embroidered with gold and silver lilies.

'I'm sorry the jewels are missing,' I said, though I was thinking of the painted birds with their bright plumage, the animals with feathered wings, and felt sad I would never be able to look at them again.

'The book will be repaired, and you need have no worry about the jewels.' He gave a short laugh. 'Whoever took them will receive an unpleasant surprise, for the gems are not real, they are just polished glass.'

He struggled to bend his back, and turning an iron key in the lock of a heavy oak chest, he lifted the lid and slowly removed something wrapped in a linen cloth. Then placing it on the altar, he carefully unfolded the bundle. I gasped, for there was a pale rose coloured calfskin cover with a gold and silver cross, surrounded with garnets and amethysts, and very like the one stolen by Uhtred.

'We knew the Eorl was searching for his mother's necklace, and thought it best to keep the real cover here. We shall ask our most gifted monk to repair the book, but for now, both shall be returned to the chest for safe keeping.'

He slipped Cuthbert's gospels inside the cover, and he was carefully fastening the clasp when a dreadful cry of anguish shattered the quiet of the church, making the air tremble. I spun round and was shocked and terrified to see Uhtred in the doorway, wild eyed, ashen faced, and his fine linen tunic torn and stained with blood.

'I thought you dead,' I cried in horror.

'Fool, do you think I was destroyed?' he shouted, striding towards me and violently thrusting the hermit aside. 'A ledge broke my fall!' Then seizing the abbot by his robe, he cried, 'Give me what is left of my mother's necklace! You cheated me, you knew the jewels false!'

Snatching the book from the abbot's hands, he ran back to the porch, but the two monks working close to the church had heard the shouting and barred the door. Raising their hoes like crossed swords they bravely faced the maddened desperate Eorl.

'There's no escape, give up the necklace,' the hermit called to him, but Uhtred turned and ran headlong down the north aisle and finding a door at one side of the altar, violently tugged it open and disappeared.

'The stairs lead to the bell tower,' the abbot said, white faced and sitting down heavily onto a bench, but already the hermit and Kendra were climbing the bell tower steps and I dragged myself after them. When I reached the bell loft, I heard their footsteps above me, and I struggled up another flight of stairs and found them at the door of the bell chamber.

'Don't enter – the platform won't bear the weight of two people,' the hermit warned, but I took no notice. Shouting I must save the holy book and keep my promise, I climbed through the door and stepped onto the narrow ledge.

Taking up most of the tower room was an enormous bell. It was suspended from a stout oak frame and hanging through the opening above the bell loft, and looking down between the bell and its frame made me dizzy. I could see Uhtred on the far side of the platform, his back pressed against the wall and the boards sagging under his feet.

'Take care!' I warned him. 'Is your mother's necklace worth dying for?'

The Eorl moved along the walkway, and under his feet, the wood had split where rain had blown into the tower for many years.

'Keep the cover – just return the holy book to me!' I pleaded.

'No!' the Eorl screamed. 'Why should I give you what you want? You took what is rightfully mine!'

'I didn't take it, your father did,' I said as calmly as I could, afraid in his anger he might kill us both. 'The monks' book means nothing to you.'

I stepped carefully along the platform, but he shuffled away from me. Thrusting his arm through the wooden slats in the narrow window spaces he shouted, 'Come any nearer and I'll drop your precious book into the stream and you'll never see it again!'

Frantic to stop him, I edged towards him, holding out my hand and crying, 'The monks gave their lives to save the book from the Northmen. I beg you – give it back to me!'

He shook his head and now he held the book towards me, just out of reach, a wicked grin on his face. His dark eyes looked mad, and his forehead had a deep cut where he must have hit the cliff when he fell. He laughed, leaning towards me, almost letting me touch the cover with my fingertips, and then jerked it away, but his sudden movement made him stumble. Trying frenziedly to recover his balance, he fell and caught as the edge of the platform. Hanging by one arm, his body dangled above the bell loft floor.

He was gripping the book in one hand and clinging to the platform with the other. I slithered down the wall onto my knees, and leaning towards him as far as I dared, tried to reach him.

'Give me the book, catch hold of the platform with both hands, save yourself!' I begged him.

His knuckles were white, his fingers loosening. Sweat poured down his face and he bared his teeth like a snarling animal. Then pressing the jewelled cover to his lips and laughing wildly, he plunged through the gap between the platform and the bell, hitting the floor of the loft below with a thud.

Horrified, and sickened to think what might have happened to him, I heard the hermit and Kendra going down the stairs, and when I reached the loft it was empty. Rushing to the bottom of the tower steps, I stumbled into the church and saw the old abbot sprawled on the paving, and the two monks bending over him.

'Stop him!' the monks shouted, 'stop the madman! He attacked the abbot!'

Following Kendra and the hermit to the porch, I saw the Eorl staggering along the path towards the mill and the monks from the long house giving chase. The fall must have injured Uhtred, for he did not get far. By the time we reached him, the monks had cornered him close to the mill and he was yelling something but it was impossible to hear what he said above the thunder of the wheel, the clanking buckets, and the roaring water.

He was screaming and backing dangerously close to the millrace, wild-eyed, and furiously looking for a way of escape. Pushing between the monks crowding round him and frantic to save the gospels, I lunged forward, taking him by surprise, and snatched the book from his trembling fingers.

Ignoring the pain in my leg, I leapt away. He stared at me in astonishment, then at the jewelled cover in my hands, and he had the look of a trapped, wounded animal. I thought he was going to hurl himself at me, but he was swaying and seemed hardly able to stand.

Time seemed to hold its breath. We looked at each other in a strangely silent, peaceful world of our own. The roaring of the water in the millrace, the monks around us, were suddenly far away, and the anger and despair in his face were gone. He smiled at me and nodded, and then turning quietly away he threw himself into the channel and the surging water carried him down into the wheel pit.

For what seemed like a very long time, I stayed frozen in the silence. Then the noise of the mill roared in my head and I felt the monks milling around me. Cold with shock, I shuffled forward and joined them at the edge of the leat. Looking down into the raging, boiling water, I watched the Eorl's limp body shoot from under the wheel, bump down the millrace into the stream, and disappear in the reed beds. Several monks set off to search for him along the bank, and trembling, and not wanting to talk, I walked silently with Kendra and the hermit back to the church.

The abbot was slumped on a bench, looking white and shaken, and when the old monk heard of Eorl Uhtred's death, he lifted his head and looked up at me and I gently placed the gospels from Lindisfarne into his lap.

'The cover will be buried with the Eorl,' he said, touching the gemstones with one gnarled finger, his voice so weak I had to bend close to hear his words. 'We shall make another for Cuthbert's book. Juliana's jewelry is tainted with too much blood. It is sad his need for his mother's keepsake was so strong he preferred to die, rather than live without it.'

Then wearily he thanked me, and although I was unhappy never see the animals and birds again, I knew the gospels would be safe. Limping after Kendra to the porch, and feeling suddenly very tired, I was just in time to see the hermit leaving the church. Calling after him, he swung round, and I glimpsed the gold cross set with garnets, part hidden in his cloak.

'Your cross, the cross you wear, Abbot Higbald wanted to know if–'

I never finished my question, for Kendra shook my arm, and turning impatiently to see what she wanted, the hermit was gone. Puzzled, and thinking he must have taken another path to the long house, I followed Kendra to the gate and said excitedly, 'Now I remember! It was his eyes, the hermit's eyes – he had the look of Widsith! The cross was the one Saint Cuthbert wore in the painting on Lindisfarne! How did he come by it?'

Kendra laughed and thumped me on the back, nearly knocking me over. 'The hermit *is* Saint Cuthbert – and Widsith too!' she spluttered. 'I wondered how long it would be before you noticed! He takes many guises when helping those who need him.'

'Why didn't you tell me?' I said, angrily. 'You knew and didn't tell

151

me!'

'You wouldn't have believed me,' she said with a toss of her head. 'You had to work it out for yourself. That's the only way you would understand.'

'He's gone, and I didn't have a chance to thank him.'

'Don't look so miserable. He has travelled with you since you set out with your grandmother from your settlement. There are few who have had such care. Be glad and think yourself one of the lucky ones, see.'

'Who are you Kendra? How do you know these things?' I asked, beginning to be afraid of what she might answer.

'I've been with Saint Cuthbert long before you were born. He brought me to Lindisfarne when your kinsfolk killed me – and my parents – in the mountain wars. After the battle, Cuthbert found me wandering in the hills and brought me to Lindisfarne. I've worked for the hermit, helping him to care for others, ever since.'

I looked at her, opened mouth, and she gave a long low whistle and Modig bounced up the path towards her. Instead of running to Kendra, the dog nuzzled my hand and looked up at me with large brown eyes and I had to fight back the tears.

'Yes it's your Bodo,' she said softly. 'He's been with me since he died saving you from the wolf. Don't you remember the strange dog on the path under the trees – the one who protected you from Uhtred's hunting pack? That was your Bodo. He was with you when you hid in the rubbish pit – you felt him lick you. It was a comfort, wasn't it?'

I couldn't answer for the tears of joy in my throat and I stroked dear Bodo's domed head and whispered his name as he looked at me lovingly. Then suddenly the full horror of what she'd said about her family came back to me. 'How could you help me when my kinsmen slew your family?' I gasped. 'How could you bring yourself to do it, Kendra?'

'It was Cuthbert. He knew how bitter I was. My heart was full of hate and I was not ready to find rest with my ancestors in the Welsh mountains. That is why Cuthbert gave me the task of looking after my enemy's son. At first I couldn't bear to talk to you, but….well, you hadn't killed anyone, so I forgave you and it brought about some healing.'

I looked at her shining eyes and didn't understand how anyone could forgive like Kendra, or be good and kind like Cuthbert. For me, living in this world often seemed a cruel and frightening thing.

'Where are you going?' I said, for she was walking away from me with Bodo as her heels and I couldn't bear it. 'Don't go – don't leave me – shall I see you again, Kendra?'

She turned and grinned at me. 'Oh, I won't be far, even if you don't see me. I'll look after Bodo for you, and if you're in trouble, just shout and I'll rescue you again. Though I think you'll be quite capable of looking after yourself in future – just keep away from the crossing place.'

'I don't want you to–'

'You'd best hurry. Fugol the messenger will wonder what has

153

happened to you. Tell him I met with a kinswoman and have decided to stay for a while.'

'Don't go, Kendra,' I pleaded. 'I shall miss you.'

'I'll miss you too,' said Kendra, 'but I must be on my way. In time, I'll be ready to move on and join my ancestors. Look, isn't that Fugol over there?'

I looked towards the trees and saw no one, and when I turned back, Kendra and Bodo were gone.

Feeling empty and terribly sad, I set off slowly down the path to the trees, shuddering as I passed the millrace. Then reaching the bottom of the hill, I crossed the bridge. Looking nervously about, there was no sign of the robbers, and thinking I'd soon be going home to my family, I began to feel better.

I wondered if Rinan had grown taller and I smiled and promised myself I would try to be less jealous of him. Then I thought of my brave grandmother, and hoped she was well, and remembering I'd killed my first wolf, I looked forward to my celebration now that I was a man. Thinking of Siward, and how he had risked his own life to save my family, I decided to ask father if my uncle and his wife Eacnung could be at the celebration too.

I found Fugol waiting for me at the inn. He was glad to see me, fearing that something terrible had happened, but I gave him news of Kendra and said nothing more. He didn't ask any awkward questions, and fetching the ponies from the stables, he helped me mount. The sun was warm on my face and the sky a clear washed blue as Fugol and I set off on our journey. The sea was calm, the waves had small white crests, and excited and looking forward to my celebration, I sang to myself and urged my pony along the road.